ISOLDE

IRINA ODOEVTSEVA

ISOLDE

Translated from the Russian by
Bryan Karetnyk and Irina Steinberg

and with an Introduction by Bryan Karetnyk

PUSHKIN PRESS
LONDON

Pushkin Press
71–75 Shelton Street
London WC2H 9JQ

Isolde was first published as *Изольда* in Paris, 1929

First published by Pushkin Press in 2019

Published with the support of the Institute for Literary Translation (Russia)

ИНСТИТУТ ПЕРЕВОДА

AD VERBUM

1 3 5 7 9 8 6 4 2

ISBN 13: 978-1-78227-477-3

Frontispiece © Anna Golembiovskaia

Designed and typeset by Tetragon, London
Printed and bound in Great Britain by TJ International, Padstow, Cornwall

www.pushkinpress.com

ISOLDE

Introduction

"No, I feel it, I know it: nowhere shall I ever again be as happy as I am here, on the banks of the Neva." Thus did Irina Odoevtseva, writing in Paris in 1967, conclude the first volume of her memoirs, an ode to her youth spent in Petrograd among the great luminaries of Russia's Silver Age, then in its twilight years. Having fled Russia in the wake of the 1917 Revolution, Odoevtseva went on to become one of the most outstanding and controversial writers of the Russian diaspora: the author of five novels, two sets of memoirs, as well as dozens of poems and short stories. Yet it was the final chapter of her life, the coda, that lent her life and art its unique fatal significance: among her generation in exile, who had for over half a century continued to dream of Russia, returning to it time and again in their art, Odoevtseva alone went back to live there. In 1987, at the grand age of ninety-one, she boarded an aeroplane in Paris, arriving a few hours later in Leningrad to find herself once again on the banks of the Neva, where untold celebrity awaited her.

Odoevtseva was born Iraida Gustavovna Heinike on 27 July 1895, to a family of Russified Baltic Germans living in Riga, then in the Livonian Governorate of the Russian Empire. A native of the Baltics, Odoevtseva was keen to hide this facet of her heritage at the earliest opportunity; she cared little for the industrial port city of her birth and in time would Russify her given name and adopt her mother's Russian maiden name in place of her father's. As a child she enjoyed frequent trips to the imperial capital, St Petersburg, where the family kept an apartment and her father, a distinguished lawyer, prosecuted cases in the Senate. With the outbreak of the First World War in 1914, the family relocated from Riga to the capital, now renamed Petrograd in concession to the rampant anti-German sentiment of the day. There Odoevtseva was married to her cousin Sergei Popov, also a lawyer and an assistant to her father. Odoevtseva later described the marriage as "purely fictive", having been arranged in order to alleviate her father's fears that after his return to Riga she would be "fed to the wolves" (that is, to her numerous suitors). She received a divorce ere long.

Odoevtseva's first tentative steps into the world of literature began in Petrograd. In November 1918 she enrolled in the literary faculty of the newly established Institute of the Living Word, which had been founded with revolutionary zeal to democratize the arts and sciences, and offered an array of lectures given by various celebrities of the era, including People's Commissar for Enlightenment Anatoly Lunacharsky, the theatre director Vsevolod Meyerhold and the children's poet Kornei Chukovsky. There, Odoevtseva honed her poetic talent under the tutelage and encouragement of Nikolai Gumilyov, a leading figure of the Acmeist movement, which held compactness of form and clarity of expression as the highest poetic ideals.

It was during Odoevtseva's time at the institute, where she took regular classes in literary studies and rhythmic gymnastics (a method devised by the Swiss theoretician Émile Jaques-Dalcroze), that she became acquainted with the stars of Russia's Silver Age—not only Gumilyov, but also the writers and poets Andrei Bely, Osip Mandelstam, Zinaida Hippius, Dmitry Merezhkovsky, Ivan Bunin and her future husband, Georgy Ivanov. Her beauty played no insignificant role in attracting this widespread attention—already for the best part of a decade, Odoevtseva had been admired for her good looks throughout the capital, known in particular for an oversized bow in her hair—but it was not without a modicum of irony that she now set this renown to work in forging her literary career: her early poem, 'No, I Shall Not Become Famous' (1918), included the provocative lines:

Neither Gumilyov nor the wicked press
Will ever call me talented.

I'm just a little poetess
Who wears an enormous bow.

Recognition of her talent came soon enough, however. Odoevtseva ensconced herself in Acmeist circles, diligently applying herself to her vocation, and eventually became a member of the Guild of Poets, which Gumilyov re-established in 1920. Public and critical acceptance followed on the back of her daring and wildly successful poem, 'The Ballad of Powdered Glass' (1919), which recounts the woeful tale of a Red soldier who, in order to feed his family, sells salt laced with the offending substance. It ends in the manner of a fairy tale, with the murderous soldier borne away and placed in a glass coffin by seven ravens before being thrown into a bog, where his body is to lie until the Last Judgement. The poem was published in the prestigious and influential *World of Art* journal, where it won Odoevtseva overnight celebrity and prompted a succession of invitations to give public readings of her verses. When Gumilyov fatefully introduced her to Ivanov at one such evening on 30 April 1920, held in honour of Bely, Ivanov's enraptured response was: "Was it you who wrote that? Can it really have been you?"

The subsequent two years proved to be some of the most emotionally intense of Odoevtseva's life. Contrasting the blissful romance of Ivanov's courtship, walks in the Summer Gardens and budding literary success were the burgeoning privations of life in revolutionary Petrograd; Gumilyov's execution for his supposed participation in an anti-Bolshevist plot; and ultimately, the death of Odoevtseva's mother. Having finally divorced her first husband in 1921, Odoevtseva married her beloved "Zhorzhik" in the September of that year. The couple lived together with their friend, the poet and critic Georgy Adamovich. It was also around this time that Odoevtseva's father returned to newly independent Latvia. The young Odoevtseva's virulently anti-Bolshevist political stance, set forth with great vigour in her verses, made remaining in Russia an increasingly dangerous prospect, as it was for the many writers, artists, politicians and intellectuals who fled the so-called "Red terror" of the fledgling regime. In the winter of 1922, the couple decided to join the general exodus of over a million Russians fleeing their homeland for Europe and the Far East, Ivanov having obtained permission to leave under the sham pretext of building a "state repertoire for theatres", Odoevtseva having adopted Latvian citizenship. Very likely the couple absconded in the same expectation held by so many of their compatriots: that the Bolshevist government would soon collapse, and before long they would once again find themselves on the banks of the Neva. But fate held something different in store: for Odoevtseva, the journey to Europe would mark the beginning of an exile that lasted sixty-five years.

After a month in Riga, Odoevtseva travelled on to rejoin her husband in Berlin, which until the early 1920s constituted the capital of Russian émigré culture. There, the couple lived in relative luxury—in sharp distinction to the majority of their more penurious compatriots—thanks to a regular income received from a rental property owned by Odoevtseva's father in Latvia. Availing herself of the Weimar capital's many delights, she led a charmed life there, taking classes in the latest dance crazes, dining in the most fashionable restaurants and cafés, attending galas and balls, as well as hobnobbing with literary grandees and visiting celebrities such as the poet Sergei Esenin and his wife Isadora Duncan. True to her calling, however, Odoevtseva would still lament that everyone "seemed to have forgotten about poetry" in Berlin. And so it was that in August 1923, she was once again swept along in the general outflow of Russian émigrés leaving Berlin because of the financial crisis, drawn by the literary lure of Paris.

Odoevtseva arrived with her husband and her father, filled with fantasies of Parisian glamour and sophistication. Her hopes were dashed from the very outset. The picture she would paint of their new home in the second volume of her memoirs, *On the Banks of the Seine* (1983), was one of abject disillusionment:

We arrived in Paris at the worst possible time… My father and I installed ourselves very unsuccessfully in

an enormous, gloomy hotel with no lift. An acquaintance of my father's had said that it was one of the best
hotels. To me, however, who was used to Berlin's elegant
pensions, the prospect of such a life seemed utterly
insupportable. We would dine in a vast restaurant that
was bleak and uncomfortable. I ordinarily dined in the
finest restaurants. We would walk along the boulevards.
By eleven o'clock everything was shut. The streets were
dark… We couldn't sleep for the racket outside. It was
not at all what we had expected.

To add insult to these material injuries—though they
were mere trifles compared to the hardships suffered by
so many of Odoevtseva's contemporaries, who found
themselves destitute and working menial jobs as labour-
ers, dockers, waiters and such—by the mid-1920s most
Russian refugees were beginning to accept the fact of
their exile as a permanent condition. Yet while the reality of Soviet rule in Russia left a bitter taste, it did not
prevent these newfound *apatrides* bearing the torch of
Russian culture. Indeed, it was not for nothing that in
1927 the poet Dovid Knut was able to claim: "the capital
of Russian literature is not Moscow, but Paris". By the
middle of the decade, the city had succeeded in attracting the great and the good among the exiled Russian
political and artistic elites, and this was the milieu in
which Odoevtseva set about making a name for herself

as she delved into prose writing. She was an habituée of the capital's most fashionable and prominent literary salons, though she preferred to remain a sideline spectator, rarely if ever partaking in their notoriously tempestuous debates. Dmitry Merezhkovsky and Zinaida Hippius, the undisputed, eccentric doyens of Russian culture in exile, hosted one such group: by dint of their celebrity status during the Silver Age—and owing also to their fortuitous ownership of an apartment at 11-bis, avenue du Colonel-Bonnet—they were able to recreate something resembling a literary salon *à l'ancienne* on Sundays in Passy. One of the emigration's most influential circles, it attracted luminaries such as Ivan Bunin and Teffi, while fostering a younger generation of writers emerging in exile, such as Gaito Gazdanov, Yuri Felsen and Odoevtseva herself.

Odoevtseva's first short story, 'Shooting Star', appeared in 1926 and a serial publication of her first novel, *The Angel of Death*, began in the émigré newspaper *Dni* the following year. Her novel was a runaway success and appeared in English and German translations in 1930. For all her literary progress in Paris, however, Odoevtseva frequently quit the city for the pleasures of the Riviera or to visit her family back in Riga. In fact, she and Ivanov temporarily relocated there in the autumn of 1932 so that Odoevtseva could spend time with her terminally ill father. After a year spent in Riga where they contributed to the local émigré newspaper, *Segodnia*, the couple returned to Paris in possession of a substantial inheritance that Odoevtseva had received from her father, with which they purchased a villa at Biarritz—a move that doubtless provoked the jealousy and resentment of their less fortunate compatriots in exile. Indeed, the ostentatiousness of the life enjoyed by Odoevtseva and her husband, coupled with Ivanov's notoriously difficult character and the acerbic criticism he published in the émigré press, would contribute by the end of the decade to the couple's ostracization from large swathes of the Russian enclave.

The war in Europe marked a tragic turn in the fate of the entire émigré community, which found its allegiances and loyalties tested to breaking point. Odoevtseva and Ivanov removed to their villa at Biarritz and continued to live there under German occupation. On the back of the widespread resentment that had built up in regard to the couple, malicious rumours of their collaboration with the Nazis now spread, devastating their reputations and turning them into pariahs among their own people. To make matters worse, these rumours appeared to have been started by none other than their erstwhile bosom friend, Adamovich. Odoevtseva later generously wrote them off as a misunderstanding. When the couple arrived in Biarritz in 1939, they hosted several charity evenings, one of which was attended by a British admiral. Felsen happened to read about this in the society column of a newspaper and wrote to his friend Adamovich, who by then had volunteered for service in the French Foreign Legion. Odoevtseva explained that Felsen's letter was delayed by several months and by the time Adamovich received it Biarritz had fallen under the German Occupied Zone: "Adamovich decided that I was receiving Nazi generals and, with his innate talent, wrote to all his friends that I was riding out on horseback with the Germans."

The damage to their reputation had been done. Former friends and acquaintances now turned their backs on the couple and would not receive them. Alexander Kerensky, the former leader of the Provisional Government and once friend, returned their letters unopened. Not only that, having enjoyed considerable luxury before the war, Odoevtseva and her husband found themselves virtually penniless by its end: the Soviet Union's annexation of Latvia and its "nationalization" of Odoevtseva's property there had cut off their principal source of income; the Germans confiscated much of their private property in 1943; and their villa at Biarritz was destroyed by Allied bombing in the latter stages of the war. When they returned to Paris, they found their apartment ransacked and their gold stolen. Dubbed *personæ non gratæ* among the diaspora, the couple sank into profound poverty. To earn money, Odoevtseva turned her hand to translating scripts into French with the help of her long-standing friend, the author Georges Bataille, and she and Ivanov would resort to hand-painting and inscribing editions of their own poetry in an attempt to make them more valuable to collectors. Their pitiful circumstances continued to deteriorate, and by 1955 Odoevtseva and her husband were forced to take up residence, despite their relative youth, in a government-funded retirement home for stateless individuals at Hyères, near Toulon. Alone, impoverished, bereft of the cultural and intellectual environment to which they had once been accustomed, their banishment was near complete.

It was not until 1958 that tragedy offered a chance for reconciliation: Ivanov's death in August allowed Odoevtseva to make peace with her fellow exiles. She took up residence in a home for the aged at Gagny, on the outskirts of Paris, and returned more actively to poetry, publishing several new volumes of verse, much of which was noted for its technical mastery. It was also there that she set about composing her memoirs; the first volume, *On the Banks of the Neva*, appeared in 1967 and, with a controversy that was by now characteristic, caused uproar among the exiled community.

In 1963, she met her third husband, the minor novelist and literary critic Yakov Gorbov, who wrote in French under the name Jacques Gorboff. Though Gorbov came from a wealthy Muscovite family, as with so many of his compatriots he had found himself in dire straits in emigration and, like a certain other émigré author, supported his literary career by driving a taxi. Gorbov had long been a fan of Odoevtseva's, even taking a copy of *Isolde* to the front with him in 1940, where both he and the book were wounded by a single bullet. (Odoevtseva would later have the tattered, bloodstained edition rebound and returned to Gorbov with a charming inscription.) The pair married only in 1978, after the death of his first wife, whom he had married in 1918 and who had been confined to a mental asylum before Odoevtseva met him.

Thereafter began the astonishing final chapter of Odoevtseva's life. In the aftermath of Gorbov's death in 1981, she found herself again in relative material comfort, bequeathed an apartment on rue Casablanca in Paris's fifteenth arrondissement and in possession of a motor car that had been fittingly gifted her by Gorbov. However, loneliness, old age and ill health began to exact their melancholy toll—until, that is, an unexpected invitation arrived in 1987. Under the Soviet Union's new era of glasnost, Odoevtseva received an offer to return to her beloved Petersburg (now Leningrad), which she wasted little time in accepting. When she stepped off the aeroplane at Pulkovo Airport, she was greeted with widespread adulation, and the ensuing press coverage and republication of her memoirs in the Soviet Union brought the nonagenarian writer a degree of celebrity that could scarcely have been hoped for at any other point in her career. As the poet Yevgeny Yevtushenko recalled,

Odoevtseva was "transported from one concert stage to another as a kind of talking relic". She was venerated as a living link to the Silver Age of Russia's pre-revolutionary past, to the poetry of Bely, Blok and Gumilyov, which for most Russians had vanished in 1966 with the death of Anna Akhmatova. More than that, Odoevtseva's grand homecoming instigated a frenzy for the "lost" literature of the emigration, which had been banned in Russia since the 1920s. It was to this end that in the foreword to the Soviet edition of *On the Banks of the Seine*, Odoevtseva addressed her new readers:

> Now I turn to you to ask that you love the people about whom I write in this book. Each one of them needs more love, not only because the "bread is bitter and the stairs are steep in foreign lands", but also because, more than bread, they wanted for the love of a reader, and they were stifled in the air of freedom offered by foreign countries… If you, my readers, fulfil my request and love those about whom I write, you will afford them temporary immortality, and me the knowledge that I have not lived in vain on this earth.

Writing thus, she did all she could to reconcile the schism that had existed since the revolution, following which so many lives, and Russian literature itself, had diverged on two very different paths: Soviet and émigré. This homage to her exiled compatriots, most of whom were now dead and with whom her relations had undergone such considerable strain over the years, was the final act of her literary life, and one of its most meaningful.

Whether as poetry, prose or memoir, Odoevtseva's writing was always a departure from the mainstream—and *Isolde* is no exception. Just as her verse written in Petrograd after the revolution was remarkable for its overt anti-Bolshevist partisanism, so, too, in exile Odoevtseva's prose fiction would chart a very different course from that of her contemporaries, winning renown and courting controversy in equal measure. In vast distinction to the elegiac, nostalgic prose of the older generation of exiled writers, Odoevtseva's maintained the grace and youthful vigour of her poetry, dispensing with the dangerous political overtones and shifting its focus to the no-less-daring realms of female sexuality and desire.

Her debut novel is a work of considerable piquancy for its time, as *The Angel of Death* witnessed its fourteen-year-old protagonist fall in love with the lover of her married older sister, with devastating consequences. Odoevtseva's even more audacious second novel, *Isolde*, appeared on the heels of this early success two years later, in 1929. A modernist reversioning of the archetypal love triangle, the mediaeval legend of Tristan and Isolde, the novel explores the competing drives of love and death, Eros and

Thanatos, amid the hermetic world of adolescents and against a backdrop of exilic trauma and despair. Despite their seemingly tender years, Odoevtseva's children, a pair of Russian-born siblings and their coevals, are on the cusp of adulthood, coy, erotically charged, and increasingly conscious of budding sexuality and the violent impulses it stimulates. With such dangerous, unmistakably Freudian overtones, Odoevtseva's children share the same perverse, reclusive universe as Jean Cocteau's "holy terrors" in *Les Enfants terribles*, which debuted in the same year.

Isolde projected, with cinematic precision, a dark, troubling vision of wayward youth living on the fringes of society, provoking vociferous outrage and polarizing critical opinion among the exiled literary establishment. Pavel Milyukov, the former politician turned scandalized editor of Paris's leading émigré newspaper, *Poslednie novosti*, condemned the novel: "It's high time to tell this talented young writer that she's heading for a dead end." Though so much remains off-stage, merely hinted at, others still called the novel deplorable, tasteless and immoral, accusing Odoevtseva of casting the gravest aspersions on the moral probity of émigré youths. The critic Mark Slonim charged Odoevtseva with abusing "sexual spice"; the novelist Vladimir Nabokov took issue with the "dry" style, the lesbian overtones and stereotyping of the English; and Kirill Zaitsev, then editor of the nationalist and religiously oriented *Rossiia i slavianstvo*, in a pearl-clutching fit of moral indignation dubbed the whole thing "frightful".

Put simply, the novel was not at all what was expected of an émigré author in terms of subject matter or style: from a Russian perspective, it was all much too modern, much too European, much too explicit, much too close to the bone. In daring to depict the criminal and sexual exploits of a group of adolescents, *Isolde* shocked readers with its portrayal of themes not only considered taboo, but also in some quarters deemed beneath the austere dignity of the Russian canon. Not since Mikhail Artsybashev's *Sanin* in 1904 had Russian letters witnessed so perturbing a treatment of sexual mores, and, even then, never before those of youths belonging to a supposedly respectable class. The arbiters of literary discernment in the diaspora, who viewed their mission primarily as one of cultural preservation in the face of the Soviet peril, were fundamentally conservative and preached the continuation of Russia's literary tradition, namely that of the nineteenth century. Yet Odoevtseva's troubled and unsettling portrayal ran counter to the classic Tolstoyan image of a golden childhood spent amid the serene, tranquil glories of Russia's past. Instead, she opted to banish her children from that Eden and thrust them into a profane world in which the trauma of their exile is a forbidden subject, in which the vanity and egotism of their mother results in their emotional neglect and abandonment, in which the dark mechanisms of their psyches are set in motion by sexuality, desire and criminal instinct. Hers is a world still reeling from the horrors of the revolution and the Great War, shimmering with the vain and hollow distractions of *les années folles*—its casinos, cocktails, dance halls and jazz bands—fully conscious of their impotence to save, let alone enrich, the lives of these unhappy children. Lost between childhood and adulthood, Odoevtseva's *enfants terribles* inhabit a liminal space, on the fringes of society and morality, a grim universe in which lurid individuals lurk at every corner, ever ready to exploit and abuse them. Far from the hackneyed, nostalgic idyll demanded by convention, Odoevtseva's vision of adolescence presented her compatriots with a disturbing glimpse into the present, bearing witness to the total breakdown and disintegration of a family with disastrous, tragic results.

For all the reactionary chill, *Isolde* enjoyed a warmer reception among the younger members of the diaspora, who discerned in it their own sense of loss and alienation, their own confused longing for a Russia that many of them did not know or, at best, remembered only vaguely. Evoking the nihilistic mood of many young émigrés, *Isolde* captured something essential of the zeitgeist. Caught between Russia and Europe, between past and present, doubly marginalized within their own marginalized community, the younger generation was inherently better placed to appreciate the diverse shades of Odoevtseva's fiction, as well as its technical and thematic leaps forward, which took their cue from European literature and intellectual thought. Immediately apperceiving its daring innovativeness in the realm of feminine perspective, the young novelist and critic Vladimir Varshavsky commented:

Despite the impropriety of bringing up sexual character in the arena of literary criticism, one is still drawn to say: until now literature has known only women as seen through the eyes of men, not the life and world as seen through the enigmatic eyes of women. Of course, there have been women writers, but hardly any of those whom I have read wrote about what they saw with their own eyes as they looked at life up close, at point-blank range. In depicting the world, they always employed intellectual assumptions shared by men, in the majority of cases invented by men, which is to say that they were playing, as it were, their roles in some obligatory theatre built by men. In… *Isolde*, Irina Odoevtseva charts out a new course for women's literature. The story of a fourteen-year-old girl's sensual perception of life and the hitherto unknown female image that emerges from it reveal to us something truly new.

It is in precisely this spirit, one of presenting "something truly new", that Irina Steinberg and I offer up this English translation of *Isolde*, the first since its original publication in Russian ninety years ago. It is our firm hope that Odoevtseva, having discovered "temporary immortality" on the banks of the Neva, will once again live awhile abroad.

BSK

London–Kiev, 2018

ISOLDE

Part One

I

"THIS IS WHAT the sea was like when Isolde sailed upon it." Cromwell shut his book and looked out over the horizon. "This is what the sea was like when Isolde sailed upon it, to Tristan."

The sky grew pink with the approaching sunset. Wave ran over wave. The wind ruffled the cotton towels laid out on the beach. Round shells glinted dimly in the grey sand. And far away in the distance, right on the horizon, a bright white sail stood out against the silky blue sea.

"This is what the sea was like…"

A seagull flew over his head with a cry, almost clipping him with the sharp tip of its wing. Cromwell flinched.

"What's come over me?" he thought angrily, blushing with embarrassment. "I'm flinching like a little girl! I'll soon be scared of mice at this rate."

He tossed the book away and turned over to lie on his back.

France was to blame. Yes, France was most definitely to blame. He was never like this at home.

He cast his mind back to the green fields of Scotland, to the castle with its grand square rooms, to Eton, where he had boarded that winter term. You wouldn't have caught him flinching there! But here in Biarritz life was completely different—mad, fun, even a little seedy. Yes, that was the word: seedy. And there was the perpetual rush of the ocean. And the bracing air. And these stupid books. And the eternal waiting, the constant premonition of love... He scanned the horizon again.

The enormous sun was lowering itself slowly into the rose-tinged waves. And the sky, as if freeing itself of the sun's weight, was becoming ever lighter, ever clearer, ever paler. Everything around Cromwell grew paler, airier, softer. The high turrets of the bathhouse faded into the misty air, the bare cliff-face grew soft mossy-blue shadows, while the grey sand glinted gently. In this crepuscular light, even the bathers in their glistening wet costumes seemed to be an extraordinary silver people, who had appeared out of nowhere and were now swimming off into the unknown.

Cromwell heard the sand crunching faintly behind him. He turned around. Isolde was walking straight towards him. Her wide white cape was billowing in the wind. Her fair hair fell around her shoulders. Her big, bright, limpid eyes looked out to sea searchingly, as if she were expecting something. She walked quickly, with a sure and light step, her neat little head held high. She was not walking, but floating through the foggy air.

"Isolde," he whispered in confusion. "Isolde!"

She seemed to have heard him. She turned her head and looked at him as she walked past. Cromwell felt a warm light on his face, as if bathed in the morning sun. He closed his eyes with a sigh. The light tripped across his face, across his shoulder and then disappeared. He opened his eyes. Isolde was gone. All around him was deserted. He was alone, lying on the hard, wet sand. He was cold. Where was Isolde? Where had she disappeared to? He stood up and looked around.

Swimmers' heads bobbed up and down in the waves, but Isolde's was not among them—he would have recognized her by her blonde hair. He quickly started walking along the beach, staring at every passer-by, but he couldn't see her anywhere. Maybe she didn't actually exist? Maybe he had imagined her? Of course, he must have done. Where could a girl like that have come from? Girls like her didn't really exist. He had spent too long out in the sun, too long dreaming up Isolde. He had imagined it all.

No, she was real, flesh and blood. He could still feel her warm gaze on his skin and hear the sand crunching under her feet. He hadn't imagined it. Surely, he hadn't seen her only to lose her straight away?

As he walked along the wide, empty beach, his heart thudded dully.

"What nonsense," he thought, consoling himself. "She couldn't have disappeared just like that. If I don't find her today, then I'll see her tomorrow. I'm getting myself worked up over nothing. And what's she to me anyway?"

He shrugged.

"She's just some girl." He thrust his hands deep into his pockets and turned back, whistling a tune. "What nonsense."

That was when he heard the scream. A desperate scream that carried across the beach. Other voices rose in reply. Frightened voices.

"She's drowned? Who is it? Who's drowned?"

"A girl has just drowned!"

People ran from all sides towards the spot where Cromwell had just been lying. He ran with them. He couldn't quite understand it, but he could already feel the weight of irreparable destitution in his heart.

She had drowned. A girl had drowned. It was her, Isolde. He ran and ran, stumbling as he went, overtaking the others.

"Isolde. Isolde has drowned," he kept repeating to himself nonsensically.

Gasping for breath, he ran up to the crowd of people gathered around her. He squeezed his way through, pushing someone out of the way. In front of him, on the wet sand, lay a girl. He fell to his knees beside her in horror. But it was not Isolde. The girl's wet hair, short and black, had fallen all over her face. Her button nose was strangely white. Her face was calm. Exceptionally calm. Even her half-open mouth and blue lips couldn't detract from this calmness and the pure, simple look on her face. Her black swimsuit hadn't had time to dry and water was seeping through it onto the sand. Her thin, childish legs were squeezed together demurely. Her arms were spread wide open.

It wasn't Isolde. Cromwell lifted his face up to the sky, took a deep breath and felt a joyful sense of release all through his body. He laughed out loud. Catching himself, he looked around—nobody had heard him.

"The doctor! The doctor's here!"

A gentleman in a grey suit kneeled in front of the girl and pressed his ear to her wet chest. Everyone was looking at him. Maybe it wasn't too late? But the gentleman shook his head and stood up again, brushing the sand off his knees.

"It's too late. Heart attack."

"Is she dead?" He saw a head pop up from behind someone's shoulder. She was wearing a green rubber bathing cap that covered her ears. Her big bright eyes narrowed in curiosity and horror.

"Is she dead?"

Isolde. It was her. He had found her. He moved towards her and held her by the elbow. She gave him the same look of curiosity and horror.

"Is she dead?" she asked again.

Her arm was trembling. She was standing beside him, so close to him, in her bright green swimsuit, which was still damp. She kept shifting from one foot to the other in agitation.

A woman was running along the beach towards them. She was fast, but unsteady on her feet. Her white skirt billowed up over her knees, revealing occasional glimpses of pink suspenders with metal clasps on her thighs. Her high-heeled shoes kept getting stuck in the sand. She was exhausted, but she kept running, all the while pressing a ball of wool with long, shiny knitting needles to her chest, as if the wool and the needles were her salvation.

The crowd parted in front of her.

Cromwell held Isolde by the elbow.

"Let's go, you don't need to see this."

She let him lead her away.

When they reached the bathhouse, he sat down on the sand. She sat down next to him.

"They should have saved her! Why didn't they save her?" Her lips were trembling. "It's awful."

"Yes, it's awful. Are you a careful swimmer? Promise me you'll be careful."

She didn't seem surprised that this boy, a stranger, was asking her to promise him something.

"I promise. But she should have been saved," she added quickly. "She was only twelve and she was an excellent swimmer. Her father just came down from Paris last night."

She threw her arms around her knees. The toenails on her tiny, tanned feet were painted with bright nail varnish.

"What does she paint them for?" The thought crossed his mind.

She kept looking back to where the dead girl lay. He could see only the back of her head, in its bright green cap, and a part of her suntanned cheek.

"How awful," she said again, but her voice was calmer this time. "Are you English?" She turned to face him. "I'm Russian. What's your name?"

"Cromwell."

"Cromwell? Are you named after *the* Cromwell?" she said, recollecting something and pointing over her shoulder, as if just there, behind her, stood all the centuries of the past.

"Yes, my namesake."

"Your parents must have known their history."

"They must have done." He smiled. "And what's your name?"

"Liza."

He shook his head.

"No, your name is Isolde."

"Isolde? Who's Isolde?"

He held out his book. "It's all in here, everything about you. You can borrow it if you like."

"This book is about me?" She opened the book and read out the title: *Tristan and Isolde*.

"No," she said quietly. "It's not about me. Isolde was a queen. But I'll read it anyway. Thank you."

They sat next to each other on the sand. The sun had already set.

"Would you give me a cigarette, please," she said.

"You smoke?"

"Naturally."

She lay back and crossed her thin legs one over the other. The smoke from her cigarette floated straight up into the sky. She didn't look like Isolde now. In her bright green swimsuit, she looked more like a grasshopper.

"No, I'm no queen," she repeated. "In fact, I'm very modern. Why do you look at me like that?"

"You ought to get dressed. It's cold now and you could catch a chill."

She jumped to her feet.

"Very well," she agreed. But he was suddenly seized by the fear that he would lose her again.

"I'll wait for you. What are you doing tonight? Do you have plans?"

"No. But I'll go home for dinner. I'm famished."

"Well, since nobody's expecting you, you can come and have dinner with me. Let's go. I have my car here."

"Your car? Your own car?"

"Yes, I got it this spring for passing my exams."

"What make is it?"

"It's a Buick."

"A Buick," she repeated, and laughed with delight. "Your very own Buick! Hold on, I'll only be a minute."

She ran up the stairs to the bathhouse, clearing two steps at a time.

He stood there, waiting for her. The dead girl was slowly stretchered away past him.

Cromwell absent-mindedly watched the stretcher and the crying woman accompanying it. It was nothing to do with him. It was someone else's grief. Whereas he—he had found Isolde!

He turned away. Of course, it was a pity. A terrible pity. But he didn't feel it. He was overwhelmed, blinded, crushed with joy.

He heard a door slam somewhere in the bathhouse. Liza emerged from one of the cabins. Cromwell looked at her intently, taking in her legs in their silk stockings, her painted lips and her loose hair.

"No, you're not Isolde. You shouldn't wear your hair down if you wear lipstick."

She blushed.

"You don't like me like this? Hand me your handkerchief." She quickly wiped her mouth, staining the handkerchief red. "You're an Englishman after all, a Puritan, a Quaker." She laughed. "But it's all right. I want you to like me. Is this better?"

I I

A TATTERED WHITE CLOUD was slowly floating across the dark, empty sky. Liza lifted her face to it.

"Look, it looks just like an angel." She paused. *"Po nyébu polúnochi ángel letél,"** she recited. "You don't understand, do you?"

He was concentrating on the road, overtaking as often as he could.

"I don't. I'll bet it's Russian, no?"

"Aren't you interested in what it means? The poem is Russian, but the author was Scottish by birth, just like you."

"It's not that I'm not interested. I just don't care for poetry, even in English."

Liza was sitting next to him. Her hair was blowing in the wind.

"The smell of your hair! It's all in my eyes. I can't see the road. We're going to break our necks because

---

* *Po nyébu… letél*: The opening line from Mikhail Lermontov's poem 'Angel' (1831): "Across the midnight sky an angel flew…"

of your hair. No, don't fix it back, I beg you! That smell!"

Liza laughed quietly.

"It smells of the sea. I'm having such fun! I'm not frightened at all."

They fell silent once again. Her knee brushed his. She leant into his shoulder.

"Well, here we are in Biarritz. Do you really want to say goodbye? If you like, we could go to the Château Basque…"

"No!" she said, suddenly alarmed. "We can't go there!"

"Why not?"

"We just can't," she said. "My… A relative of mine is performing there tonight," she added shyly.

But he was English, so he didn't ask any more questions.

"So, where shall we go?"

"I don't know. But I don't feel like going to any restaurants. What about the lighthouse, shall we go there? Lovers always go to the lighthouse, and you're in love with me, aren't you?"

He looked at her earnestly.

"Yes, I'm in love with you, Isolde."

"Really?"

The car was cruising along the dark ring road. It was deserted and quiet. The street lamps were unlit. The houses, with their shutters closed, seemed asleep.

"Are you really in love with me? How nice! I'm so happy!"

Her face grew pensive, almost sad.

"But you know, if you're really in love with me, I have to tell you something. I have a boyfriend. He's in Paris right now."

Cromwell recoiled.

"Oh, I see…"

But Liza quickly took his hand.

"You've got it all wrong. It's nothing. You can still be in love with me. I like you a lot." She looked at him shyly. "Kiss me."

He shook his head.

"But it doesn't even mean anything! You're being so silly. Kissing is so lovely."

She put her arm around his neck.

"Please, kiss me."

The car drew to a halt.

"Look, here's the lighthouse."

He helped her out of the car.

She walked along beside him, trying to peer into his eyes.

"You're angry, aren't you? Don't be angry with me."

The lighthouse momentarily lit up her blonde hair and pale face, the edge of a bench, someone's knee, someone's lips.

Cromwell and Liza walked on in silence. She stopped and stood right by the edge. The wind blew out her long skirt and loose hair. Her lips were ever so slightly parted. She looked out at the waves with a sad, melancholy air, as if she were expecting something.

"Now you look like Isolde again!"

She kept looking out to sea. It was as if she hadn't heard him. Her skirt was beating noisily in the wind, like a flag. She stretched out her arms. The thought crossed his mind that she might take off with the wind. But she lowered her arms helplessly, as if she were folding her wings.

"What have I done wrong?" she said, with a note of sadness in her voice. "I haven't done anything. Please, don't be angry with me."

"I'm not."

She gave him her hand and he squeezed her cold fingers.

"Kiss me," she pleaded.

He bent down and kissed her on her cold lips. She sighed deeply and closed her eyes.

"I just wanted to show you that I'm not a child any more," she said shyly.

III

Liza opened the door to Nikolai's room.

"Kolya! Kolya, it's time for coffee!"

Nikolai was standing in front of the mirror, doing up his tie. He turned to face his sister, visibly annoyed.

"What time did you get in last night?"

"Not at all late. Anyway, you should be pleased with me, not cross. Feel free to congratulate me—I have my own motor car now!"

"And where did you come by that?"

"An Englishman has fallen in love with me. He has his own Buick. And what's his is mine. He's rich. You should see how much cash he carries in his wallet!"

"You're not lying now, are you, Liza?"

"No. I'll introduce you today, if you're nice to me. Anyway, let's go!" And she ran ahead, clearing two steps at a time.

They drew to a halt in front of a large white door.

"Listen, Kolya, don't say anything to *her*, will you?"

"As if I would!"

Liza knocked on the door and immediately, without waiting for an answer, flung it open. She ran into the room and jumped on the bed.

"Good morning, Natasha!"

Natalia Vladimirovna freed her arms from under the embroidered sheets and embraced her. "Good morning, my little bird! Good morning, Kolya."

She kissed them both tenderly. Liza kicked her feet up in the air, threw back the cover and got into bed beside Natalia Vladimirovna.

"I want to go to beddy-byes!" she said in a babyish voice and kissed Natalia Vladimirovna. "I want to go to sleep next to Mummy!"

Natalia Vladimirovna looked around her in alarm, but the door was closed.

"Can I?" shouted Kolya. "Nobody can hear us. I want to sleep next to you too, Mummy!" He got onto the bed too and threw his arms around her neck. "Liza gets everything, what's left for me?"

Natalia Vladimirovna was laughing and protesting.

"Oh! Be quiet! Won't you be quiet, my little darlings! Please!"

But they paid her no heed and carried on clambering all over her, kissing her. Only when the maid brought in the coffee did Liza and Nikolai move over to sit on the edge of the bed. Natalia Vladimirovna poured for them.

"Mama, I want the coffee froth," Liza said in a babyish voice and Natalia Vladimirovna spooned some out for her, smiling contentedly.

"Here you go, my little bird, you can drink it now."

"Mama, give me your biscuit! Yours is nicer."

Natalia Vladimirovna laughed and gave up her biscuit.

"How are you, my little darlings?" she said, patting Kolya on the head. "Do you like it here? Have you been doing lots of running around and catching crabs on the beach?"

"Mmm hmm, catching lots," he said, his mouth full.

Someone should really have explained to their mother that there was no crab-catching to be done in Biarritz, for there were no crabs. But she never went to the beach and her understanding of how her little children spent their time there invariably involved them catching crabs. Her little children, who always went to bed at nine on the dot, right after reading Andersen's fairy tales. And yet, they were really monstrously big, her little children. They aged her terribly. She could never for the world admit that they were her own. No, they were orphans and she was their cousin. That's why she was raising them.

Liza reached out for the sugar bowl and accidentally knocked her arm on the table.

"I've hurt my elbow, Mummy, it really hurts!"

Natalia Vladimirovna stroked her arm and kissed it better.

"There you are! Now it doesn't hurt any more, Liza darling. Your elbow doesn't hurt any more. As for that table, let's spank it, so it doesn't dare hurt my little Liza again!"

On the armchair beside the bed, Liza spotted a pink nightdress. She held it in her hands and stroked the delicate, rustling silk, quite lost in thought. Her eyes narrowed with pleasure.

"Mummy, can I have this?" she asked haltingly.

"You want the nightdress? But whatever for?"

Liza blushed.

"Please, Mummy, I really want it!"

"But what do you want it for?" said Natalia Vladimirovna. "Do you want it to sew a dress for your dolly?"

"Yes, yes!" Liza agreed happily. "A dress for my dolly! One with lace."

"Have it if it pleases you."

They heard a knock at the door.

"May I come in, Natasha?"

Natalia Vladimirovna quickly glanced at her children and conspiratorially held a finger to her lips.

"Come in, Tanya!" she said.

Tanya Solntseva strode in. She was a friend of Natalia Vladimirovna's.

"You haven't forgotten, have you, Natasha? We're having lunch with Grünfeld today, and Boris will be there too. He asked me to tell you—"

"Tell me later!" Natalia Vladimirovna interrupted, casting a pointed glance at Liza.

"Oh, your little cousin." Solntseva patted Liza on the head. "Such a graceful little thing, like a young gazelle! If I were you, I'd definitely put her into the ballet school. Look at that little face!"

"Nonsense, stop it," said Natalia Vladimirovna, screwing up her face in annoyance. "Liza shall finish school and then marry. No ballet."

"As you wish, you strict cousin! Let her marry." Solntseva sat down in the armchair, crossed her legs and lit a cigarette. "By the way, Liza, how is that little friend of yours, the good-looking one, with a falcon-like air about him?"

Liza blushed.

"Andrei? He's in Paris."

"A pity. He's charming. You must know it, of course. I'm sure you're in love with him."

Natalia Vladimirovna nudged her friend.

"Tanya, what ever are you saying! Liza is a child!"

"Oh, please! Look at this child's eyes!"

As though afraid that her eyes might betray her thoughts, Liza quickly lowered her eyelashes and gazed at the pattern on the rug.

"He's delightful, your little falcon-boy. So wild, so melancholy. It's a pity he's so young. How old is he?"

"Sixteen."

"Ah, yes, too young. A couple of years from now, perhaps." Solntseva stood up, laughing. "Two years from now I'll definitely try to steal him away from you. But you'll have left him long before then anyway." She gave Natalia Vladimirovna a kiss. "I must be off. Goodbye, Liza darling. Goodbye, Kolya."

Natalia Vladimirovna sighed.

"Thank God she's gone. Don't listen to what she says, Liza darling. She's quite unhinged. It's too maddening—I only get to see you two for an hour in the mornings and even then we're constantly interrupted."

A car horn sounded outside. Liza ran up to the window.

"Natasha, it's Bunny."

"Bunny? Pass me my mirror, Liza darling," Natalia Vladimirovna hurriedly fixed her hair and applied some powder. "He's the last thing I need first thing in the morning. Go, let him in, Kolya. I do hate when he starts scratching at the door."

Abraham Vikentievich Rochlin, who went by the nickname Bunny, was already making his way up the garden path. He was uncommonly short. His stumpy little legs, clad in dainty yellow boots, took cautious, uncertain steps along the sandy path. His pale round eyes bulged and glinted behind his pince-nez. The look they had was at the same time cunning and somehow abashed.

"May I come in? She isn't asleep, is she? She isn't angry with me?" he asked shyly.

"Good morning, Bunny dear!" Liza offered him her hand. "Natasha is already awake."

He shuffled in sideways, holding his hat and a cigar in his hands.

"Good morning, Natalia Vladimirovna, did you sleep well?"

Natalia Vladimirovna sat up, making herself more comfortable on the pillows.

"Oh, it's you!" she said, in a cruel, mocking voice. "And where were you yesterday? Did you bring it?"

"I did, I did!" As he gingerly reached for his wallet, he dropped his cigar on the floor.

"Stop making a mess." Natalia Vladimirovna frowned. "Throw that cigar out the window. Give me the wallet. Children, go out and play."

"That's not all of it." Bunny wiped his forehead with his handkerchief. His clean-shaven round face convulsed fearfully. "She's angry. Please God, have mercy," he whispered.

"Out, children!"

Kolya and Liza left. Liza ran to the terrace, stomping her feet as hard as she could. She stood there for a minute before creeping back to the bedroom door on her tiptoes. The key was in the lock and she couldn't see a thing. She placed her ear to the keyhole. Natalia Vladimirovna was saying something very quickly and angrily. Then something made a loud noise. What was it? The wallet hitting the wall or a hard slap?

"You! You! No, it's you!" Bunny squealed in a high-pitched, womanish voice.

Liza clasped her hand over her mouth and ran out into the garden, laughing.

"Bunny's getting it in the neck!" she shouted, laughing uncontrollably.

Nikolai was sitting on the swing next to Liza's friend Odette. Odette turned to Liza. She had a suspicious look in her eyes.

"What's this Kolya's telling me? Who were you with last night?"

Liza shrugged.

"What's it to you? Are you jealous?"

"Not in the least. But who is this Englishman? Where did he come from?"

Liza hopped and turned on one leg.

"If you know too much, you'll grow old too soon."

Odette bit her bottom lip in disappointment. Liza nudged her.

"Don't be cross. We're going out tonight. I'll take you with me and you can ask him all your questions, all right?"

Odette nodded, but her brow was knitted.

"Come on, cheer up! Kiss her, Kolya, she's in love with you."

"Nonsense. You're imagining things."

"Cromwell's already waiting for us. I have to change out of this get-up." Liza lifted up her leg and showed them the short stockings and sandals she was wearing. "Come on, Odette, help me get changed."

"Don't put too much slap on! It looks ridiculous with your hair. You'll look obscene!" Nikolai shouted after them.

"That's none of your concern, you'd better look after yourself," Liza snapped back.

Nikolai remained in the garden and thought about the one thing he always thought about when left to his own devices—where and how to get his hands on some money. He needed money to have fun. Without money, life just wasn't worth living.

Having fun meant going out to restaurants, buying ties, playing cards. Having fun meant living. Without money, life just wasn't worth living.

But there was no money. The fifty francs' pocket money he received was hardly money. But now that Liza had found this Englishman… Well, that could be interesting.

Nikolai pushed himself off with his foot and swayed there slowly.

"What's taking them so long?" he thought irritably.

IV

CROMWELL WAS WAITING for them on the beach. Liza introduced them: "This is my brother, and this is Odette."

Cromwell shook Nikolai's hand heartily, baring his white teeth in a broad grin.

"Delighted to make your acquaintance. Wasn't it splendid weather for swimming today?"

"Indeed," said Nikolai.

"I played tennis this morning."

"Is that so?"

"I won six–two."

Nikolai tried to look interested.

"There's polo tomorrow," Cromwell persisted. "Do you play?"

"No."

"What about cricket?"

"No."

"Basketball?"

"That's also a no."

"Well, football, then. You must play football."

"I'm afraid I don't play football either."

Cromwell looked crestfallen.

But the disappointment soon passed. After all, Nikolai was Isolde's brother. Of course, had he been an Englishman… But he was Isolde's brother, a creature almost as mysterious and magical as she. So he could be forgiven for not even playing football.

The four of them went to the casino. But Liza wasn't allowed in.

"No children."

"This always happens with you." Nikolai was angry. "You always ruin everything."

Liza felt guilty.

"You can go on your own, or with Odette. We'll wait."

"Go on my own?" he retorted in Russian, scoffing at the very idea. "With what money? It's all because of your hair. And I was sure to win today. You won't be let into the restaurant either, mark my words."

They sat out on the terrace of the casino. A waiter approached them.

"I'll have a cocktail," said Liza. "Which one? I don't mind which, so long as it has straws."

Odette nodded.

"I'll have the same."

Cromwell drank whisky.

"Lovely weather, don't you think? Though it is rather hot… They say that Russians are first-class riders." He really wanted to say something nice to Nikolai.

Nikolai laughed.

"That may be so, but I've never sat on a horse."

"No, really?"

Liza leant in to speak to Cromwell.

"Wouldn't it be much nicer on our own?"

"Yes! Tomorrow it'll just be the two of us."

"Tomorrow?" Liza looked over at the neighbouring table, dreamily. "Crom, tomorrow is so far away."

Nikolai jabbed her with his elbow.

"See, everyone's staring at you again. It's your hair."

Liza shrugged him off.

"Leave me alone." And she leant in to speak to Cromwell again. "Crom, you haven't kissed me once today."

Later that evening they went out to an expensive restaurant. Odette self-consciously studied the stiff white tablecloths, the flowers and the chandeliers that shone too brightly. Liza smiled serenely. She liked everything, especially the music and the women in their evening gowns. She was positively beaming with pride. It was, in essence, she who was treating her friend and her brother to a night out.

"Don't be shy," she said to Nikolai in Russian. "Order whatever you like."

"We must drink to our friendship! Shall we?" Cromwell poured champagne for everyone. "To a real friendship, a friendship that will last for ever, in life and in death."

Liza clinked glasses with him first.

"I'll only drink to life," she laughed. "But—our whole life."

Cromwell held his glass out towards Nikolai.

"Then you and I must drink to death."

Nikolai laughed too.

"When it comes to champagne, I'll drink to anything!" They clinked glasses and he drank. "Are you having fun, Cromwell, old chum?"

"In spades!" Cromwell nodded enthusiastically.

"Yes, such fun!" Liza clapped her hands.

"Be quiet, everyone is staring at you as it is!"

Liza shook her head.

"They're staring because I don't look like anyone here, because I'm Isolde."

It was late by the time they set out for home. Cromwell was at the wheel, while Kolya and Odette sat in the back. At a sharp bend, Liza turned to them.

"Listen, you two…"

But they weren't listening, they were kissing. For some reason, Liza found it distasteful.

When they reached Odette's house, Nikolai clambered out of the car after her.

"I'll see her across the garden and then walk myself home. It's just a stone's throw from here."

"Goodnight!" Cromwell shook his hand. "See you tomorrow. And don't forget our friendship in the morning!"

"Of course not. Goodnight."

Cromwell started the engine.

"Five more minutes," Cromwell kept saying. "Just up to that house, see there, and then the tram stop."

Liza would agree wearily but happily. They drove around like that until daybreak. Liza sighed.

"What a shame it is to say goodbye! But I'm practically asleep. Goodnight, Crom!"

She opened the gate and entered the garden. A long black shadow darted across the path.

"Who's there?" Liza cried out in fright.

"It's me, it's me."

"Bunny? Is that you? What are you doing here?"

"I'm waiting." Bunny sat down on the bench. "I'm waiting for Natalia Vladimirovna."

"I expect she must be singing at the Château Basque right now, you should go there."

"I'm not allowed to."

"Why not?"

"She forbade me. Come and sit with me, Liza dear."

Liza sat down next to him.

"Aren't you cold, Bunny?"

"Of course, I'm cold. But it's all right, it's all right. I'll catch a cold, then pneumonia, then I'll die and she'll be ashamed of herself."

Liza laughed quietly.

"You're like a schoolgirl, Bunny."

But Bunny wasn't listening.

"No, she won't be ashamed, will she? She's shameless. Shameless, cruel and base. That's right—base. Oh, how she torments me!" Suddenly he was sobbing. "Base! She's there with her lover, that Boris. While I have to sit here. Oh, Liza dear, if only you knew!" He started wailing, shaking uncontrollably.

"Please, Bunny, please, don't cry."

He rested his head on her shoulder, still sobbing.

Liza gazed into his round, flaccid, sorry face. She knew that she should be offended on behalf of her mother, but the very sight of him was so pitiful. He was crying. While Natasha was singing, with everybody listening and admiring her. He was here, and she was far, far away.

Liza put her arms around his neck.

"Don't cry." She tried to console him, stroking his thinning hair. "My poor little Bunny, poor little fluffy Bunny. My lovely, quite remarkable little Bunny."

"She's devious, devious!" he sobbed.

Liza dabbed his face with her lace skirt. As usual, she didn't have a handkerchief in her pocket. He was beginning to calm down, and only now and again sighed pitifully. His head rested heavily on her shoulder.

"Bunny dear, I must sleep. And so should you."

"No, no!" he interjected suddenly. "She's not devious, no! She's wonderful, kind and noble. She can do anything. She's proud. She's the Queen of Sheba. She must be worshipped. Worshipped!" He stood up straight, while his puffy round eyes bulged with an unhinged stare. "She's a saint! A saint! You must love her, Liza. Love and obey her. I don't deserve her. How can I dare judge her? If she wants a lover, so be it."

Liza had grown quite bored.

"Bunny dear, do go home."

"Home? Very well." He turned on his heels and bounded down the garden path, without saying goodbye.

"Don't say a word about this to her!" he shouted over his shoulder as he opened the garden gate and shot through it.

Liza looked up at the waxing moon hanging above the tips of the pine trees. It seemed to be gently swaying. She let out a deep sigh, partly from tiredness, partly from sorrow, and went into the house.

"Sleep, I need to get some sleep. It must be six already and Kolya's still with Odette."

She undressed and lay down in her bed. Damp air was coming in through the window. The rustling of the trees merged with the dull rush of the ocean.

Liza rested her head on the pillow and thought she could see stars circling the transparent sky like great, white, luminous butterflies.

"Cromwell," she whispered and fell asleep, smiling.

She heard the door open. Someone walked into her dream. Into her dream and into her bedroom.

Liza opened her eyes and looked at the figure with her bright, vacant eyes.

"Are you asleep?" asked the unknown but very familiar voice.

She wanted to reply but lacked the strength.

"Why are you staring at me like that? Don't you recognize me?"

"I do," Liza whispered, barely moving her lips in her sleep.

"So who am I? Andrei?"

"No, you're someone else."

Sleep weighed heavily on her head and she couldn't make anything out.

"So who am I then? Who? Answer me."

Liza lifted her head, slowly coming round.

"You're Nikolai Nikolaevich Coffee-Pot," she said with some difficulty.

"Coffee-Pot? Splendid. Now Coffee-Pot is my new surname. And yours, too. Hello to you, Elizaveta Nikolaevna Coffee-Pot." Nikolai shook her arm violently.

Liza opened her eyes wider. Nikolai leant over her.

"Wake up, Coffee-Pot!"

What Coffee-Pot? What did he want from her? Why was he laughing? Liza rubbed her eyes. She was quite awake now.

"Stop it, Kolya. What is it?"

But Nikolai went on laughing.

"You're lucky you weren't born in mediaeval times. They would definitely have burnt you at the stake, for being a witch. And they would've been right, too, you green-eyed witch."

"I'm a witch and you're a coffee pot." She sat up. "Once upon a time there lived a brother and a sister, a coffee pot and a witch. One day, the coffee pot said to the witch, 'Boil me!'" She laughed out loud. "You're right, I'm a witch. Look at my birthmark." She unbuttoned her nightdress. Underneath her barely formed breasts was a dark triangular birthmark. "See? They say witches always had birthmarks." She lay back down and pulled the cover over herself. "Where have you been all this time?"

Nikolai shrugged.

"Odette wouldn't let me leave. It was so dull."

"She loves you. And no wonder! What a handsome thing you are."

"You're only saying that because I look like you."

"No, that's not it. I would have fallen in love with you if you weren't my brother."

"Of course, you would have—you fall in love with everyone. It wasn't so long ago that you were pining for Andrei, and now it's this Cromwell chap."

Liza blushed.

"You don't understand a thing."

"What's there to understand? You've fallen in love with an Englishman."

Liza shook her head.

"No, no, I love Andrei. Cromwell... Cromwell is good-looking and fun. He has a car. I like him. But..." She clasped her hands to her chest. "Oh, I can't explain it to you!"

Nikolai sneered.

"Don't worry. What do I care anyway? Fall in love with whoever you like. Look, it's gone six already. I'm going to sleep, and I suggest you do, too."

With that, he left the room, closing the door behind him.

V

LIZA FELT SOMETHING cold press against her neck and woke up with a startled cry.

"What, what's going on?"

It was already light. Sunlight was streaming into the room. Nikolai was standing over her bed. He was dressed in his pyjamas and holding a pair of scissors in his hand.

"What?" Liza said again.

"What? Take a look in the mirror."

Liza sat up. She rubbed her eyes with her fists and suddenly saw strands of her long blonde hair lying on the pillow. They were arranged in quite a particular fashion, each lock separate. They looked like live snakes, shiny and coiled up in the sun. Liza stared at them, not quite comprehending what had happened. Then she felt the back of her head with her hand.

"Kolya!" she cried out. "How could you? What have you done, Kolya?" Tears streamed down her face.

He put his arm around her.

"Come on, Liza dear, don't cry. You're far more beautiful like this. The long hair—it was getting absurd."

She pressed her face into his shoulder and cried.

"How could you! I loved my hair, I was so proud of it!"

"You would have had to cut it soon anyway. You didn't want to do it, but now it's been done for you. You're going to be a grown-up soon…"

"I'm never going to be a grown-up," she said.

He laughed.

"What do you mean, you'll never be a grown-up?"

She pressed her face into the pillow and sobbed violently.

"Why? Why did you do it? How could you?"

Three days later, Liza wrote a letter to Paris:

My darling, darling Andrei! Something terrible has happened to me. Kolya cut my hair off. I cried and cried, although it does suit me. But I'm so upset! When I had long hair, I was Isolde. That's what Cromwell calls me. He's an English boy I met here. There's a book about Isolde. I'll bring it back with me and you can read it for yourself. Cromwell is rich. We go out every day and have lots of fun, but I feel sad without you. When I'm out swimming and the salty water gets in my mouth, it makes me think of us kissing. I lie on the sand with my eyes closed and pretend you're lying next to me. I feel so sure you're there that I reach out to touch you. But you're never there, and that makes me cry. A girl drowned out here recently…

VI

CROMWELL'S MOTHER had just returned home.
"Three in the morning... He'll be fast asleep," she thought, quietly opening the door to her son's bedroom.

But the room was empty and the bed hadn't been slept in.

"Where could he be at this late hour?"

She turned the light on, sat down in an armchair and picked up a magazine.

She wasn't worried. The idea that some misfortune could have befallen her son didn't even occur to her.

She leafed through the pages of the magazine absent-mindedly. She wasn't reading, she was thinking. She was thinking about her life and about her late husband; he had been killed in the war. He had been so tall and so cheerful, with a dazzling set of teeth. She smiled at her reminiscences of him in exactly the same way that she used to smile at the man himself. Cromwell was turning out to be just like his father. As her thoughts shifted to her son, she contemplated him with as much devotion as she had afforded her husband.

The door silently swung open, and Cromwell walked in.

"How late you are, Cromwell!" She smiled and laid the magazine to one side. "Did you enjoy yourself?"

He blushed.

"Thank you, yes."

"I stayed up just to wish you goodnight. Sleep well, Cromwell. I'm glad that you like it here."

She got up and gave her son a kiss.

"There's something I wanted to ask you, Mama." He blushed a deeper shade of red. "It's very nice here, but *devilishly* expensive. And I…"

"Is it really that *devilishly* expensive?" She laughed. "Do you need money? How about five hundred francs?" She gave him another kiss and made as if to leave, but paused in the doorway. "You're not playing baccarat, are you, Cromwell?"

"No, Mama."

"Please don't. I'll give you the money in the morning."

He stepped towards her.

"There's something else. I'd like to go to Paris on Tuesday, on my own."

She shook her head.

"No, Cromwell darling. You know full well that we're going to Paris in two weeks' time, on the first of October. You're not going there any earlier. Please work around that."

With a slight bow she left the room.

VII

I T WAS NOON. A fierce rose-coloured sun stood high up in the brilliant sky. White waves were surging and crashing one after another. Bathers were jumping up and down, while holding onto a rope. The sound of music drifted down from the casino, its syncopated rhythms barely discernible.

Liza was lying on the hot sand next to Cromwell.

"Crom, give me your hand. Are you unhappy?"

"Why should I be unhappy?" he asked.

"Why? Because I'm leaving."

"True, but two weeks from now I'll be in Paris."

She sighed and paused in thought.

"So much can happen in two weeks. Perhaps two weeks from now, Paris and Biarritz will no longer exist. The road to Paris will no longer exist. We shall no longer exist."

He laughed.

"Where would it all go?"

"It would disappear, turn to dust, vanish into thin air. And even if it all stays where it is, it won't be the same. It could very well be better, but it would never be the same as it is right now." She shook her head. "No, it won't be better. It'll be worse. Things always get worse. Haven't you noticed that, too?"

He said nothing.

She turned to lie on her side, nearer to him, drawing her naked legs up to her torso. The wind was blowing her short blonde hair in every direction, making a halo around her head.

"Oh, Crom!" she sighed. "I don't want to leave you."

She stood up, wrapped herself in a fluffy robe and walked down to the water's edge.

"You know, I want to swim far, far away, until I'm too tired to swim any farther, and drown. Just like that girl, remember?"

She looked out across the water.

"Isolde!" he called out faintly before walking over to her. "Isolde, are you crying?"

She said nothing.

"I love you so much," he said, breathless with emotion. "Don't cry, Isolde."

She turned to him, her face happy, smiling.

"Oh, for goodness' sake, don't be so wet! It's all non-sense anyway." She threw her robe down onto the sand. "I'll race you to the rock. On your marks, get set, go!" And she threw her arms into the air and ran into the sea, splashing as she went.

VIII

IT WAS THE NIGHT of Liza's departure. They were at the railway station: Cromwell had brought her a bouquet of roses, Odette—a large bar of chocolate. Liza carried the flowers in her arms and smiled absent-mindedly, just like Natalia Vladimirovna—save that Natalia Vladimirovna's absent-mindedness was merely for show. In fact, her white-gloved hands were trembling, and the corners of her mouth twitched.

"Say," she whispered to Solntseva, who was standing beside her. "Where is he? It's almost time."

"He'll be here, don't worry. He promised you'd leave together, didn't he? Don't upset yourself. People might notice…"

Natalia Vladimirovna fixed her hat and again smiled absent-mindedly to all those who had come to see them off.

"Well, I'm sorry to be leaving!" she announced, as if she were on the stage. "I've had such fun!" She paused. "And I'm terribly afraid of railway disasters!"

All of a sudden she looked frightened. She blinked

and blinked again, as though she were on the verge of tears. Everyone hastened to reassure her.

She paid them no notice and just stood motionless by the window, tearing petals off the flowers.

"He won't make it now. Tell him, Tanya… Oh! Liza, get on! Quickly!" She interrupted herself. "The train's about to leave!"

"Farewell, Crom." Liza held out her hand.

"No, not farewell. Until next time!" He kissed her hand. "It's only ten days."

The train pulled out. Liza was standing beside Nikolai in the vestibule, waving her handkerchief and laughing. Natalia Vladimirovna turned her face away from the window. A tear rolled down her cheek. Liza cried out in alarm.

"Natasha!"

She hadn't seen her mother cry in a long time. Natalia Vladimirovna drew her shoulder back irritably.

"Leave me alone," she said, before going through to her compartment.

Liza shot a confused look at her brother.

"Why is she crying?"

"Boris hasn't come with her. He had a space reserved in her compartment. That's why she had Bunny take the morning train." Nikolai shrugged and leant out the window. "She tried so hard, only for him to pull a fast one. She's hurt." He laughed. "Anyway, let's go and take our seats in second class. We're far enough from her admirers now, so they won't witness us getting moved out of the wagon-lit. Let's go."

But the door to the vestibule opened again.

"Liza," said Natalia Vladimirovna. "Stay with me tonight. You can take the top berth. It's free. I'll pay the extra fare, don't worry. I don't want to be alone tonight. Kolya, you may go. Goodnight."

Liza walked into the compartment, still pressing the flowers to her chest. Natalia Vladimirovna had already removed her hat and coat. Her face was pale and visibly upset.

"She's not pretty at all." The thought suddenly struck Liza. "I'm better looking."

"Go to bed, quickly. No chatting. I have a headache." Natalia Vladimirovna gave her daughter a kiss. "Up you go, little bird."

Liza undressed and lay down on top of the cool sheets. She had to take care, lest she go flying off the berth. Then she'd be a real little bird! She pressed her back against the wall and set the flowers down beside her. It was a good thing that Boris hadn't come, otherwise she'd be rattling around in second class now, trying to nod off, with Nikolai jabbing her in the ribs. It was so comfortable here! She stretched out, delighted.

"Go to sleep now, I'm turning out the light. And, please, don't make any noise."

It was almost pitch-black. The only light was a tiny blue lamp embedded in the ceiling directly above her.

Liza buried her nose in the flowers, and then she remembered the chocolate! She took the bar out from under her pillow and carefully tore off the wrapper.

"Chocolate with hazelnuts, my favourite!"

The roses gave off a sweet, heady aroma. The sweetness of the chocolate tickled her throat.

The carriage rocked gently from side to side. Liza listened to the rhythm of the wheels. "Where to? Where to?" they were asking, seriously and insistently. "Far, far and away, far, far and away," hurried the rods in reply, each rushing to speak over the other.

Liza sighed. Here she was on the train, while with every passing minute Cromwell receded farther and farther into the distance. She kissed the flowers. "Cromwell," she sighed. "Crom."

Beneath her, she could hear sobbing, muffled by the noise of the wheels.

Natasha was crying. Liza looked warily over the edge of her berth. Natalia Vladimirovna was lying with her face to the wall. She could just make out her shoulders shaking ever so slightly.

Liza lay back and pressed her cheek into the pillow again. The flowers smelt just as heady and the chocolate was just as delicious, but Liza's shoulders started shaking ever so slightly, too, just like Natalia Vladimirovna's.

"Poor Natasha." But the pity she had for her mother was immediately rechannelled to Cromwell. "He must be at home now. He'll be sad. He must be thinking of me. Poor Crom." She sighed and put another piece of chocolate into her mouth. "Darling, darling Crom! Things always get worse," she recalled saying. "It's true—things always get worse."

Her heart clenched with a terrible premonition. Something awful, something inevitable was going to happen. A chill crept up her legs. She could hardly breathe.

But the wheels pounded ever more regularly, and her eyelids grew heavy as they lowered themselves over her tired eyes.

IX

Liza was awoken by an almighty jolt. Their carriage kept lurching and swaying from side to side. The engine's shrill whistle pierced her eardrums. Liza lifted her head and looked around. Where was she? She smiled sleepily. She was on a train. She was going to Paris, to Andrei. She drew up her knees and rested her head on her arm, basking in the snug warmth. Something tickled her cheek. Ah, yes, it was the flowers. She pushed them away and they fell to the floor with a soft rustle.

"Never mind. I'll be in Paris soon, with Andrei." She lay there, smiling to herself. The pillow clung to her cheek unpleasantly. Liza felt its dampness. Why was it damp? Surely, she hadn't been crying? Surely, she hadn't been upset and afraid? No, not her, not Liza! What was there to be upset about? What was there to be afraid of? After all, she was going to Paris, where Andrei was waiting for her.

Natalia Vladimirovna touched her shoulder.

"Get up, Liza darling, we're nearly there."

Liza sat up and dangled her naked legs off the edge of her berth.

"See, we've made it without any accidents."

Natalia Vladimirovna's eyes were puffy.

"Didn't you sleep well, Natasha?"

"No, I have a migraine."

"So, when you've been jilted by a lover, it's called a migraine. I must tell Kolya," thought Liza, kicking her feet in the air.

"I slept wonderfully! I'm so glad to be back in Paris. Aren't you?"

Natalia Vladimirovna was powdering her face in front of the mirror.

"Quickly now, Liza, get dressed."

Liza looked out of the window. Were they nearly there? Nearly? Now a tall wall with big black letters across it drew into view: "PARIS".

Liza clapped her hands.

"Mama, Paris!"

Natalia Vladimirovna turned to glare at her.

"How many times must I tell you not to call me 'Mama'! Don't forget our umbrellas and your flowers."

Liza glanced down at Cromwell's flowers. It wasn't worth taking them—they had already wilted. She kicked them aside and stepped out into the corridor.

The train drew to a halt. Liza was first to jump down onto the platform. Andrei, where was Andrei?

But Andrei was nowhere to be seen. In vain she scrutinized the crowd of onlookers. Nikolai alighted from one of the second-class carriages. He looked drowsy and irritated. He gave Liza a mock bow.

"Did you sleep well, Your Highness?"

"Leave me alone."

The three of them clambered into a taxi. A cold, driving rain pelted the car windows. Umbrellas glistened in the streets. Nikolai shivered.

"What a cold reception Paris has given us! What's the matter with you, Liza? You should have had a good night's sleep."

"I have a headache. And so does Natasha. So you can cut your prattling."

In Auteuil, in their little pink villa with its large windows, the maid and Bunny were already waiting for them.

"Did a telegram arrive?" Natalia Vladimirovna asked as soon as she walked through the door.

"No, *madame*."

Natalia Vladimirovna proceeded straight to her room, without bothering to remove her hat. Bunny remained in the parlour, standing quite awkwardly in the middle of it.

"What are you doing out there?" she shouted. "Do you need an invitation?"

Liza washed and changed. Heavens, how long it all took.

"Kolya, why do you suppose he didn't come to meet us?"

Nikolai was busy unpacking.

"Who, Cromwell?"

"Don't be so stupid—Andrei."

Nikolai shrugged.

"He must have overslept, your Andrei."

"Overslept? He couldn't have overslept."

"Then he must have fallen under a tram."

Liza stomped her foot.

"Be quiet!"

Nikolai laughed.

"As if I'd be scared of you! You're like an angry kitten. Come on, hiss at me!"

Liza ignored him and quickly put on her gloves and coat.

"If *she* asks, tell her I've gone to Odette's."

"All right, all right. Go, she won't ask. She's got other things on her mind. She's having it out with Bunny now, and afterwards she'll either have a fit of hysterics or go to her dressmaker's."

Liza ran out of the house and carried on running all the way to the end of the street, without stopping once.

"What if he's fallen out of love with me? Or died?" she thought, climbing the stairs. "What if he's not at home?"

Andrei's aunt opened the door.

"Liza darling, are you all back already?"

Liza curtseyed politely.

"Yes, we got back this morning. Kolya sent me to ask if he could borrow Andrei's algebra book."

"Come in, come in. Andrei is ill. He's got a sore throat. Andrei, you have a visitor."

She pushed open the door and Liza saw Andrei. He was lying in bed, covered up with a red blanket. His hair was dishevelled. A chequered sock was tied around his throat.

"He must have taken it off his left foot," thought Liza.

He turned his gaunt face towards her and blushed deeply.

"Liza? You mustn't see me like this. Step outside for just a moment and I'll make myself presentable."

Liza held out her hand.

"Hello. I'm so happy to see you. I thought that——"

He shied away from her hand.

"Wait, let me get up."

"Please, you needn't."

"All right, you two, I have things to do. You stay here and talk," Andrei's aunt said before leaving the room.

Liza looked at Andrei, at his worried face, at the cover hanging off the bed, at the disarray in his room. All of it—his illness and his worry, the crumpled shirt he had on, the impoverished surroundings—made her heart clench with tenderness.

She laid her hat on the chair.

"Andrei, my poor darling!"

"So that's what your haircut looks like! It really does suit you."

She sat down on his bed.

"We haven't said our hellos yet."

"No, wait, step outside for just a minute. Let me get dressed. I'm embarrassed to be seen like this."

She held him close.

"You've lost weight. And your eyes are so sad! Did you miss me?"

"Awfully."

"I missed you too. Oh, Andrei, I couldn't wait to come back. But just look at you—you're so sad." She sighed and said, "'*Et alors, parce qu'il était toujours triste, on l'appela Tristan.*'* That's from that book about you and me. You're Tristan and I'm Isolde."

Andrei frowned.

"What about that Englishman?"

Liza shook her head.

"The Englishman doesn't exist any more, it's over."

"Really?"

She nodded.

"I swear."

They heard his aunt call from the hallway. "I must be off now! If anyone rings, please answer the door, Liza dear!"

They heard the front door shut. Andrei laughed.

"As if we'd ever open that door! Come on, Liza, give me a minute and I'll get up properly."

---

* *Et alors… Tristan:* "And so, because he was always sad (*triste*), they called him Tristan."

She placed her hands on his shoulders.

"Don't you dare. You're ill, so you must stay in bed. And to save you embarrassment, I'm going to get into bed with you. Hold on." She quickly threw off her coat and shoes. "There. Now you've nothing to be ashamed of." She threw back the cover and got into bed beside him. "You know, when Tristan was dying he called out to Isolde, but she couldn't get to him in time. She sailed to him aboard a ship, but he was already dead. And so she lay down next to him, placed her arms around him and died too. Close your eyes and come closer to me. Don't say anything. Just like that. That's how they lay there, both of them dead."

Part Two

I

Bunny rushed out of the building. He had a startled, slightly unhinged look about him. His bowler hat was askew and tears were streaming down his face.

"Fifty francs! Fifty!" he kept repeating in astonishment. "Me! Fifty francs!"

He threw out his stubby arm, as if to push something aside, and broke into a run along the pavement, tears still streaming down his face. At the corner, he stopped suddenly, remembering that his taxi was waiting, and turned back.

"To the Claridge," he said to the driver.

The usual thoughts raced through his head. "The window on the left side is open. I ought to close it, it's a bad omen." But he didn't close the window, he just shook his head helplessly. He didn't have time for bad omens when everything, absolutely everything, was going to hell in a handcart.

"Fifty francs! To me! Me! A man to whom Witte himself once paid his respects."

Bunny sat up straight. His round blue eyes flashed under his pince-nez. "That's right, Witte! And not only Witte! Just last year, in London… And now—a mere fifty francs!"

His eyes darted this way and that. "That's who you were then, but who are you now? What do you have?" he whispered to himself in a mocking lament. "They wouldn't lend me a thousand francs. Only fifty, with no obligation to repay. As if I were a beggar! So what's to happen now? What's next?" He drew in his neck, as if bracing himself to receive a blow. This was the beginning of the end. This is what he had been afraid of. He had fooled himself into thinking that everything was all right, that everything would be fine, but it hadn't been fine for some time now. Not since that very day, that very hour, when he met Natalia Vladimirovna at the Deauville races. His stable, quiet existence had ended there and then, and the hitherto solid ground beneath his feet had turned into an abyss.

"An abyss," he repeated aloud, drawing his feet up in alarm, as if his small lacquered shoes were not resting on the grey mat covering the taxi floor, but rather hovering precariously over death and despair, over a terrifying abyss. The very abyss he had feared all his life, which had yawned open so unexpectedly under his feet.

The taxi drew to a halt. Bunny started in surprise, but quickly composed himself, fixed his bowler, smoothed down his jacket and for some reason put on a pair of bright yellow gloves. He then twisted his lips into a scornful, indifferent smile, and calmly, confidently strode into the lobby of the Claridge. It was the kind of calm confidence that a lion tamer adopts when walking into the lion's cage.

"Pay the driver," he instructed the doorman over his shoulder.

The doorman's sharp, angry gaze tracked him for a moment, like a bloodthirsty lion ready to pounce on his tamer. His clipped moustache bristled. But he nodded obediently, doffed his gold-rimmed cap and turned on his heels in the direction of the taxi.

By that time, Bunny was already going up in the lift.

"Oof, got away with it that time," he whispered to himself. But that was the easy part. The hardest part was still to come.

He screwed up his face. "I want to do good, but all my life I've been treading the path of evil. I'm not a bad man at heart… I'm a man of the Sixties, after all. How did it all come to this?" Pity for his wife made his throat tickle. "But what am I supposed to do? What if she refuses? What if she doesn't let me have them? No, she wouldn't dare. I'll force her." He clenched his stumpy fingers into a fist. "I'll force her! I'll put her through a meat-grinder if I have to! That's right, a meat-grinder!"

He knocked on the door forcefully.

"Come in!" his wife called out.

He stopped in the doorway. His wife was playing the piano. She didn't turn to look at him, but he knew that she could see him in the mirror.

"Fanny," he said. "I wanted to ask you…"

She carried on playing, as if he weren't even there.

"Fanny, listen to me!" He tugged at his collar as if it had suddenly grown too tight. "Can't you stop playing for just one minute, for God's sake! I don't want to shout."

The playing ceased abruptly. His wife turned around and looked at him in just the same way as she had been looking at the score. The expression in her big, kind, bulging eyes—the eyes of a dairy cow—didn't change. They wore a look of fear. The fear had set in as soon as Bunny had entered the room.

"What is it?" she asked quietly.

"I wanted to ask. If you could…"

Her broad round face blanched. Her full shoulders, clad in a black woollen dress, began to tremble.

"I wanted to ask." He tugged at his collar again. "It would only be for three days. Three days only…" He lost his train of thought. "Give me your earrings!" he suddenly blurted out in a pleading, high-pitched, womanish voice.

Immediately, she raised her hands to her ears.

"It will only be for three days. There's a hitch with the business. While the money from Berlin is clearing. You needn't worry." He was speaking much more calmly now.

She was trying to take off her earrings, but her hands were shaking too much. The locks of her grey hair kept getting tangled in the diamonds.

"Just a moment, just a moment," she kept repeating in bewilderment.

"It will only be for three days… You needn't worry so much, Fanny."

At last she managed to take them off and held them out to him in the palm of her trembling hand.

He took them and kissed her hand, which was still shaking.

"Thank you, Fanny. You've been a great help. Don't wait for me to have dinner, I'll be back late."

He bowed before taking his leave. In the hallway, outside, he paused.

"I've robbed her. That was all she had left and I've taken it. What's she doing now behind that door? Is she crying?"

He felt a sudden urge to go back in, to get on his knees before her, bury his face in her stiff black skirts and beg for her forgiveness.

He closed his eyes. "I'll give her back the earrings. I will." His hand was already on the bedroom door when he heard the piano start again. The playing was confident, calm, considered. No, an unhappy woman could not play like that.

He replaced his bowler hat and bounded down the stairs as fast as a rubber ball. Once in a taxi, he lit a cigar and drew on it with pleasure. "Good job that Fanny doesn't suspect a thing. At least she won't suffer that way. Natasha will be so pleased! To think—another minute and I might have given the earrings back! What a weakling. And to call myself a man of the Sixties!" He smiled to himself in amusement.

II

Bunny returned home late. His wife was already asleep in their vast bed. He tiptoed past her into the bathroom and switched on the light. A large mirror on the wall showed him a reflection of his squat figure in a bowler, holding a cigar and wearing a tie that was slightly askew.

Ordinarily, upon meeting himself like this, he would bow deeply. "Good day to you, Abraham Vikentievich. How is life treating you?" he would ask himself and then reply with some polite little gesture. "Excellently, thank you. Still hopping around."

But today, as though ashamed of himself, he quickly turned away from the mirror and set about turning on the nickelled bath taps.

"It's a bad business. Bad. Very, very bad."

Water noisily filled the white bathtub. That sound—the sound of running water—always made him think of Imatra. Even now he could vividly picture the thundering waterfall cascading down, the silver icy water scattering the sunshine. He saw grey pines, rocks and himself, too, in his student's cap.

He undressed and lowered himself into the steaming hot bath. For a moment he was completely at peace—he had no worries, no shame, no fear. It was as if his worries, shame and fear had dissolved in the steaming hot water and evaporated somewhere beyond those white tiled walls. His stress and anxiety were replaced by a blissful feeling of exhaustion. His head suddenly grew light and empty, and rolled to rest on his shoulder as his eyelids gently closed.

If only he could stay there for a long, long time. For ever. So that there would be nothing else.

What if he were to slit his wrists in the bath? They say it's the nicest way to die. You don't feel a thing, only a sweet exhaustion, a lightness, just like now, and then you die peacefully. And that's the end of everything. He started. "No, no, I can't. It's quite impossible. I don't own a razor," he remembered with relief. He always went to a hairdresser's for his shave and didn't even have a safety razor at home. Thank God he didn't.

The water cooled. He felt uncomfortable and anxious. He wrapped himself in a bathrobe.

It isn't true, he thought. *Femmes fatales* are not sultry and dark-skinned with eyes like shining coals and full of demonic intrigues. A woman like that would not have ensnared him; he would have known how to deal with that sort. No, the *femme fatale* was blonde, grey-eyed and helpless. She loved nothing, wanted nothing. She hadn't even been cruel. No, she had been indifferent. She wasn't happy with the earrings at all today. And he had placed so much hope in them!

He lifted the bed covers and lay down next to his wife. He could just about make out her pale face in the darkness. Tresses of her long hair curled on the pillow, like damp seaweed. He moved away from her, right to the edge of the bed. The quilt weighed heavily on his chest.

So it was night-time again. Oh, what a bad business it all was!

He closed his eyes and stretched out on his back. Tomorrow… No, it was best not to think about tomorrow. Everything was at sixes and sevens—it was so difficult and so ghastly.

He suddenly remembered something his old Jewish grandmother used to say to him. She was a tiny woman, hunched over and always wrapped up in a large chequered shawl. "God forbid, Abraham dear, that you live through all the suffering that it is within man's capacity to live through."

God forbid. But God had not forbidden it. He hadn't heeded the old woman in her chequered shawl. Bunny truly felt as if he had lived through almost all the suffering that was within man's capacity to live through.

The curtains in the bedroom were slightly ajar, and a thin streak of moonlight cut across the rug. The armchair loomed dark against the window.

The piano shimmered in the corner of the room. It was warm and quiet. Fanny's breathing was barely audible.

He suddenly felt very afraid. He tried closing his eyes again. What was going to happen next? What suffering was there left to live through? Surely, not public humiliation, court and prison? No, the very thought was inadmissible. He had to lie on his back and think of something soothing. Like the stars. Stars were soothing. Starlight took two hundred years to reach the Earth. Or he could think about Egypt… No, stars were better. He just had to concentrate in order to see them clearly. The Big Dipper. Cassiopeia. Saturn. Saturn? How many rings did Saturn have? Was it nine? The rings spin slowly. What meaning did his life have, or his grief? What was the meaning of life? Saturn. Venus.

He heard something rustle next to him. He turned his head and stared into the darkness in surprise. What was it? Wasn't he alone? Alone with his grief under the starry sky.

"Fanny, are you awake?"

The rustling turned to whispering.

"Yes, Abraham Vikentievich, I'm awake."

"What is it? Did you have a nightmare?"

"No, I didn't sleep at all. I…" She let out a loud sob. "I know. You took the earrings to give to her." She was crying now, loudly, catching breaths between her sobs, just like a child. He could hear her old, wet lips parting and coming together again. "I know everything. I have done for a long time, since spring. I didn't want to say anything, but I can't do this any more. I can't, I can't, I can't!"

He leant over her and reached out his hand to touch her warm, naked shoulder. The long-forgotten sensation of her skin made his heart leap with tenderness and pity.

"Fanny, Fanny," he whispered desperately. "Forgive me, Fanny. I'm a scoundrel. I've ruined us. I've robbed us. Listen, Fanny. That's not the worst of it. They could throw us out of here tomorrow, out onto the street. How will we live? I don't even know if I'll be able to support you. And your music! You won't have a piano any more, Fanny."

Tears streamed down his sagging cheeks. He sought salvation in her shoulder as he pressed his face into it.

"Fanny, I'm so unhappy. Forgive me. Forgive me, please."

But she wasn't listening to him. She carried on sobbing.

"I knew back in the spring. And when you left for Biarritz. And I didn't say anything, not once."

Their tears seeped into the pillows, mixing together. Fanny's warm arm embraced his neck.

"What have I done to deserve this? Haven't I been a faithful wife to you? Haven't I loved you all these twenty years?"

"I don't know, but you may even have to get a job. The thing is—I've nothing left."

"I loved you so much. I love you so much. What have I done to deserve this? And who have you betrayed me for?"

He wasn't listening to her. Her shoulder, her arm, emitted a familiar warmth, one he had known in childhood.

His puffy tear-stained eyelids were closing. His puffy tear-stained lips were whispering, "Forgive me, Fanny, forgive me."

His desperation and pain had disappeared. He felt quiet, calm and light. He felt like it wasn't Fanny lying next to him, not his wife, but his grandmother, and they had wrapped themselves up in her chequered shawl. It smelt of cinnamon and onions. And it wasn't Fanny sighing and sobbing at his ear, but his grandmother teaching him in her monotone voice:

"Man must not lie. Man has a small head. He'll lie and then he'll forget what he's lied about. Not like a horse. A horse has a big head. A horse can lie if it wants to."

III

CROMWELL JUMPED OFF the tram and made his way down the street. He turned a corner and came face to face with a pink villa that was surrounded by golden autumnal linden trees. It was a small building, two storeys high, with sweeping windows and a front terrace.

Cromwell felt his heart clench, as though some misfortune lay in wait for him there.

"Perhaps I should turn back?" The fleeting thought crossed his mind.

But it lasted only a moment. He placed his hand on the gate and looked up at the window on the upper floor—her window. He felt excited and nervous. She was waiting for him just there, behind that window. He rang the doorbell. A maid opened the door.

"Is the young lady at home?" he asked.

The maid pointed to the staircase.

"She's upstairs."

"Please, let her know I'm here."

But she had already turned her back on him.

"I haven't time to let her know," she said over her shoulder. "You can tell her yourself."

Cromwell was left standing in the large, dark hallway. He could see a bouquet of wilted chrysanthemums reflected in a mirror. A grey silk overcoat was draped over a wicker armchair. A trace of perfume lingered in the dusty air. On the side table, next to the vase, he spotted a white glove. It looked like a white severed hand. The hollow fingers pointed upwards ruefully, as if they were trying to push something away.

Cromwell stared at it. Was it pushing him away, barring his way with a curse? He smiled to himself, checked his hair in the mirror and walked over to the spiral staircase. A narrow skylight lit up the white banister and the red runner. He spotted a tiny brocade shoe lying on one of the stairs. "Like Cinderella's slipper," he thought. "I wonder who lost it on their way back from last night's ball?" Was it that beautiful lady he met at the railway station in Biarritz, or Isolde?

He could hear laughter coming from behind one of the doors. He knocked.

"Come in!" shouted Liza.

He pushed the door open. The room had a low ceiling. A plush blue rug covered the floor. Evening sunlight flooded the entire space. Liza was sitting on the edge of a low divan.

"Crom!" She jumped to her feet, her blue dress fluttering

like a butterfly in the sun. "Hello, Crom! Oh, what fun!" She was holding a glass in her hand and her eyes were shining brightly. Her tousled fair hair looked like a halo around her head. "Oh, Crom, how good of you to come!" She laughed and fell back on the divan, kicking her legs up high as she went.

Nikolai slapped Cromwell heartily on the shoulder. Andrei greeted him politely, but coolly.

There was a bottle of port on the table. Odette poured him some.

"Drink this, hurry and catch up with us!"

Liza lay on the divan with her arms spread wide open.

"Oh, what fun!" she kept repeating.

Cromwell sat down beside her. As always, he felt a little uncomfortable in the company of these loud, boisterous foreigners. He considered them all to be foreigners, except Isolde. Isolde was like him. She came from the sea, just as he did. Liza lifted her head up.

"Well, where are we going for dinner then?"

"To a Russian restaurant!" cried Odette.

"I want to go to one that has music." Liza sat up. "Let's go! I just need to change my stockings. I've torn these ones." She pointed to a hole just above her knee. "Get some for me, will you, Odette? They're in the dresser over there."

Liza removed her stockings. Cromwell started at her petite legs and her feet with the rose-coloured nail varnish on her toes. Her golden sun-kissed skin gave off a warm glow. Her knees were smooth and shiny. Cromwell blushed.

Liza kicked her feet in the air.

"I love going barefoot!"

"Yes, in Biarritz…" Cromwell began.

Liza turned to him.

"In Biarritz? You know, it all seems so long ago now. I feel like I wasn't even there. I hardly remember anything. Just the sea… It's such a shame you weren't there with us, Andrei. Maybe next year…"

She pulled a new pair of stockings over her legs and fastened the clasps.

"All I need now is my shoes and then I'll be ready!"

Her discarded silk stockings lay in two small bundles on the blue rug. They were still warm, like the corpses of two small birds that had just been shot.

"I know you're a Quaker, Crom, but I'm going to put on lipstick. This is Paris after all!"

Odette was fussing in front of the mirror.

"I've already had too much to drink. See, my nose is shining and no amount of powder is going to cover it up. Just look! How am I supposed to go out for dinner now?"

Nikolai finished the bottle.

"Now we can go!"

Cromwell sat still, taking it all in—Liza darting around the room, her brother, Odette, Andrei. He had a peculiar feeling of embarrassment, joy and anxiety all at once. He felt as if already he had no right to be sitting there, no right to be listening to Liza's laughter. Since this would probably be his last time there, since he wasn't going to be invited back tomorrow, the room and all the people in it seemed to him so extraordinary and so wonderful. He looked at Liza and his heart grew heavy. He didn't feel as if he was really sitting beside her, but rather as if he were long gone, long dead, and it wasn't him, but his soul that was looking at her. His soul, which had floated out of his body and was now looking down from the sky, through the ceiling. It was passionate, desperate, it wanted to take everything in and commit it to memory. It had only a minute to do so, and thereafter lay eternity. Eternity, when he would never see Isolde again.

Liza put on Natasha's hat and her fur coat with the big stoat collar.

"I'm ready."

She opened the door and ran out. Cromwell caught up with her on the staircase. She was standing in the half-light of the window.

"Why are they taking so long?" she asked in a whisper.

He wasn't surprised that she was whispering.

"Isolde, I love you," he whispered back.

She let out a sigh and her face grew melancholy.

"Oh, why bring all that up now? You should stop…" She shook her head.

Odette and Andrei were noisily making their way down the stairs.

"What's the matter with you, Liza? You spend an hour getting ready and then you can't even wait two minutes."

They went out into the garden.

"Where's your car?" Liza sounded surprised.

Cromwell blushed.

"It's in the garage. There's a problem with the engine."

Liza screwed up her face.

"What a nuisance! I hate taxis. Will it be fixed soon?"

"Absolutely, by tomorrow!"

…A vase filled with carnations stands on top of a white tablecloth. Beside it is a glass filled with long straws. The lighting is both cheerful and mysterious. Where is the light coming from? It's streaming in from behind the mirrors and from crevices in the ceiling and from somewhere else that's completely hidden from view.

"It's hot in here." Liza pushes her hat to the back of her head which makes her face look childlike, like that of a little girl who has been running around in the garden. "What fun!" She smiles.

Odette is drinking champagne, tilting her bobbed head all the way back with every little sip.

"Yes, rather!" she says.

Liza places both elbows squarely on the table.

"We're having lots of fun, all of us, together. It's lovely. All these people here—I bet they're not having half as much fun as we are. Let's drink to us!"

She clinks glasses with Odette. Andrei forces a smile as he holds out his glass to clink with Cromwell's.

Odette points her fork at him.

"Jealous," she says in Russian.

Liza elbows her. "Be quiet."

Nikolai is saying something. He's telling some story, but nobody is listening to him.

Liza feels happy. She closes her eyes a little. It's all rather lovely. The mysterious light and the shrill music. Liza trains her ears. So that's what it's like, this jazz. It's fun, loud, snappy and ready to pop with joy! But somewhere in the background she can hear the bitterness and the sadness. It's quite audible, it isn't drowned out by all the rest. So that's what it's like... Well, so it should be. That makes it even more fun! Her head is spinning slightly, lending extra clarity to her thoughts. It is as if all her senses, her sight, her hearing, have become acutely sharp all of a sudden. She can distinctly make out a conversation three tables away, where a lady in a white dress is saying to her companion:

"That's impossible. We can't be apart."

And his answer:

"Oh, just leave it, will you? I must go."

The lady in white looks ever so sad and her eyelashes begin to flutter. Liza wonders whether Odette can hear them, too, but she can't be bothered to ask.

If she were to think of the past, her thoughts would form a triangle and fly out the dining room, right through the wall and into the street. This triangle would encompass everything she was thinking about, all the right memories. Thus, if she were to think of Mama, there'd be a nervous Bunny, and Boris, and the sound of Mama's voice. Mama laughing and Mama crying. Mama singing 'Dark Eyes'. Mama putting on her new earrings. And it's all crystal clear, and she feels so much pity for her. But she mustn't think of that or she'll get upset. It's all clear. Life. Love. The motor cars that keep pulling up outside the restaurant. And those two women with their brocaded cloaks, walking in with an air of grace mixed with nonchalance. Those poor women. They think they're beautiful. They think that everyone's admiring them. But they're ridiculous. Liza could barely stop herself laughing right in their faces. She turns to face away from them and realizes that someone is squeezing her knee under the table. Whose hand is that? Andrei is sitting next to her. Cromwell is across the table. She doesn't try to figure it out. She doesn't care. She just likes the hand there. She smiles and looks up at the dimly lit ceiling.

"How fun! How lovely!"

She removes her hat. Her fair hair falls over her face, covering her eyes like a net. It's as though everything is in a mist, which is even nicer.

Nikolai talks so much. And Odette, too. They talk too much. She can't feel the hand on her knee any more. Why did it go? It felt so lovely there.

Liza lifts up her head.

"I want to dance."

Andrei and Cromwell both jump to their feet. Their eyes meet.

Odette claps her hands.

"So now you're rivals! And you must fight a duel!"

Liza gets up too.

"I'll dance with you, Crom."

She edges carefully around the table. Her head is spinning and she could easily trip and fall. She makes it to the centre of the room. The parquet is shiny and everything is spinning. Liza, too, is spinning. Her short blue dress fans out as she dances, but she doesn't care.

It's so easy to dance, so much fun! The music is marvellous, so joyful and so sad. Her head is spinning.

"Hold me closer or else I'll fall. Oh, is it really over? I want to dance again!"

They sit back down at their table.

"Now I'll dance with you, Andrei." Liza smiles. "Tonight is such fun! I want to have dinner like this every night."

A tall Englishman in tails enters the restaurant. He stops in surprise when he sees Cromwell and regards him coldly. He makes his way past them to an empty table by the window. Cromwell turns bright red and jumps to his feet.

"Crom, where are you going?" Liza grabs his hand.

"That's… That's Leslie, my cousin. I must speak to him."

Cromwell quickly goes over to the Englishman. Even the tips of his ears are burning red with anxiety. Liza stretches out her neck. She wants to hear what they're saying, but the music is deafeningly loud. But does it really matter what that puffed-up Englishman has to say?

"Let's have a dance, Andrei."

And now everything is spinning once again, and her skirt is fanning out, and her heart keeps stopping, keeps dropping into her stomach.

Cromwell is already back at their table. He's still bright red and there's a folded cheque on a small dish in front of him. Odette looks angry and annoyed.

"Are we leaving already?" Liza sits down on the banquette. "I don't want to go just yet."

"We have to. Leslie said he'll tell my mother, so…" Cromwell blushes a deeper shade of red.

Liza shrugs her shoulders.

"So? Let him."

"If he does, I'll be sent back to London."

Liza lets out a sigh.

"How idiotic. We were having such fun! What's it to him anyway, that English goblin!"

She gets to her feet. Andrei passes her the coat with the stoat collar. Liza wraps it around herself, regards herself in the mirror and shakes her head.

"We were having such fun."

She makes her way slowly towards the exit. People are staring at her. "She's so pretty!" she hears someone say. She pauses at the door to wait for the others. Turning her head, she looks straight at the Englishman in a tail-coat.

He is looking back at her coldly, but his expression is one of outrage. He is holding the menu in his hand and a waiter is standing over him, frozen in a polite bow. But the Englishman is ignoring him. He is waiting for Cromwell to leave.

Liza bows to him mockingly and then opens her mouth to stick out her tongue at him. It all happens so quickly. She's already in the hallway. She only just has time to hear someone in the restaurant start laughing, and the sound of applause.

"You're mad," Odette whispers to her.

Andrei takes her arm.

"Well done, Liza, you stuck up for us."

Cromwell is silent.

"So, where to next?" asks Nikolai.

Odette waves her hat in the air.

"Onwards and upwards!"

It's cold. Cars drive past them, one after the other.

"So, where to?"

They stand and look at each other. Odette laughs.

"Where to?"

"Unfortunately… I… we…" Cromwell sounds embarrassed. "We can't go anywhere."

"What! Why?"

Cromwell pauses before answering, as if weighing up his words.

"I don't have any money," he says quietly.

"No money?" Nikolai can't believe his ears. "But—"

"I don't have any money," Cromwell says again. "I've just spent the last I had. I pawned my motor car today, so I can't get any more. And now, to top it all off, I've run into Leslie!"

Nikolai walks up to him and stands very close.

"What about your mother?"

"She won't give me a franc until Christmas."

"Until Christmas?" Nikolai lets out a long, derisive whistle and throws his arms out wide. "Until Christmas!"

Liza wraps the fur coat more tightly around her. Her arms drown in its sleeves. It's as though the conversation passes her by, doesn't concern her.

"It's so cold," she says absent-mindedly. Nobody answers. They are all still standing on the pavement.

Nikolai raises the collar of his coat.

"Well, what can we do? We have to get home some-how. I hope you can drop us off?"

Cromwell nods.

"Yes, yes, of course." He hails a cab. "There are five of us. I'd better sit next to the driver."

But Andrei gives him a gentle shove.

"Climb in with us. There's space for everyone."

They drive down dark, empty streets. Nobody says a word. Cromwell gazes at Liza.

They've almost reached her house. She won't invite him in. He has less than five minutes left in her company. She won't invite him in with her. If she were to say, "Maybe you could come in," no matter how coldly, even if she added, "but it's getting late," he would agree. He wants to be in her home, in her room, just one last time. He wants to look into her eyes with the lights on, wants to sit beside her on the divan.

She sits with her back to them, staring out of the window. Her hat—the hat with the white feathers—has fallen to the floor. Cromwell picks it up and replaces it on her lap. She doesn't even turn to look at him.

"Do you feel sick?" Odette asks her.

Liza scowls.

"I feel sickened."

The taxi draws to a halt. Liza climbs out first. Her face is pale. She holds her hand out to Cromwell.

"Goodbye. I imagine you'll be going straight home. We're all frightfully tired. Goodnight."

Odette also says her farewells to Cromwell.

"Thank you," she says.

"Whatever for?" he asks, abashed.

"For a fun evening." Odette smiles, before giving him a nod and running after Liza.

Liza is already making her way up the staircase. The large fur coat drags over the stairs. Her fair hair glimmers dully. She looks both miserable and regal.

"Goodnight."

"Goodnight."

Andrei and Nikolai head into the house. The door slams shut. Cromwell is left on his own. He lets the cab go. It's better to walk, in case he doesn't have enough money.

Cromwell stands in the middle of the deserted street. What is he supposed to do now? Oh, yes, he must go home. He cannot just loiter at someone else's garden gate all night, with his hat in his hands, like a beggar. He dons his hat. He must go home. After all, he knew it was going to end like this. He was expecting it, wasn't he? But still… She didn't even look at him, as if he no longer existed. Well, he doesn't exist any more. Not now that he can no longer entertain her and her friends. He walks down silent, unfamiliar streets, as trees gently rustle in gardens and the sky gradually grows light.

He casts his mind back to the day when he first saw Isolde. How happy he was before he knew her! How happy he was, without even realizing it.

As he thinks of that day, he recollects the sand, the waves, the sunset. All of a sudden, quite vividly, he sees the girl who drowned. He sees her black wet bathing suit and her dead white face. He sees her closed eyes.

Suddenly he feels sorry for her, for the first time. Back then, when he was so anxious and scared for Isolde, he hadn't had the time to spare a thought for her.

"That poor girl! That poor, poor girl!"

She had such a lovely, honest, calm face. She wouldn't have behaved like Isolde. No, she was different.

The pity he feels allays his own misery for a moment, but only for a moment.

"Isolde!" he says aloud, before bursting into tears.

"What's come over me?" he thinks desperately. "I'm crying! I'll soon be scared of mice at this rate."

He wipes his eyes with his hands. The sky has grown quite light. The wispy grey clouds allow glimpses of pink to shine through.

Cromwell lets out a sigh and lifts his face up to the sky. He sees the face of the drowned girl looking down on him, pale, transparent, dead. She's right there, just above him, glowing amid the cold dawn of the Paris sky. Transparent, bright, almost happy. Silently, she radiates comfort. Her pale lips smile at him, and her smile shines brightly.

It grows even lighter. The clouds melt away into the dawn sky. Her face turns faint and misty. No longer is it possible to make out her closed eyes and her thin eyebrows. Everything has faded. Only her smile remains. And now that smile too has disappeared. But up there, in the pink sky, where the dead girl's face had once been, a shimmering light lingers on for a long, long time.

IV

THE LESSON had just ended. Liza took off her black pinafore. Beside her, Odette was slowly placing books into her satchel. She was very pale and had dark rings around her eyes. Liza nudged her with her elbow.

"What's made you so dull all of a sudden?"

"I feel wretched. I have such a headache."

"Some fresh air will do you good. And make sure you eat a gherkin when you get home."

"A gherkin?"

"That's right. Kolya always has one after he's been out. It's the best remedy."

Their teacher walked over and pressed her hand against Odette's forehead.

"Do you have a fever? There's a flu epidemic, you know. You've been playing outside without a coat again, haven't you? You must take better care of yourself!"

Liza laughed quietly.

Boisterous schoolgirls piled out of the classroom, shouting and pushing each other as they went. They took their time getting dressed in the corridor. Liza pulled on her short navy-blue jacket with gold buttons and put a childish little hat on her head without even glancing at herself in the mirror. Here she was just a girl, a schoolgirl, so that's how she had to behave.

She curtseyed to the class teacher.

"Goodbye, *madame*."

The teacher smiled at her benevolently. "If only all our girls were as good as this little Russian."

Outside, Liza took Odette's arm.

"Well? Do you feel better?"

"A little."

"Just don't forget the gherkin. And if that doesn't help, dilute some smelling salts and take ten drops."

They heard dark, thin Angèle shouting: "Are you going home already? Jacqueline and I want to go to the fish museum."

"The fish museum? What's that?"

"Come and see for yourselves."

Jacqueline placed her hand on Liza's shoulder.

"Oh, do come with us," she pleaded. "It's always fun when you come. Come on, Liza, it's really not far, just by the Trocadéro."

Liza nodded.

"All right, if you really want me to."

Georgette linked arms with Liza.

"Yesterday, I went to the zoo to look at orang-utans.

They were so big and sad, just like real people. I felt sorry for them. But the lions were funny. They have giraffes, too. What about you, Liza, what did you do?"

"Odette and I went to the cinema."

Odette raised her eyebrows in surprise and took a deep breath of the damp autumnal air.

"We saw a really marvellous picture. There was a restaurant and dancing. Everyone was getting drunk and kissing each other. It was so racy and thrilling. Then one of them ran out of money, so everyone went home and locked him out. The actresses were wonderful. The actors, too," Liza smiled. "One of them in particular. He was so dark and looked a bit like a bird."

Jacqueline's eyes lit up.

"Racy? Did they get into bed?"

"No, there wasn't a bed, but there was knee-stroking under the table."

"Really? Which cinema was this?"

"La Motte-Picquet, but last night was the last showing."

"Did it end well?" Angèle interrupted.

"Of course! One of them married the dark boy and the other one married the brother."

Odette clapped her hands.

"Oh, Liza, you are wonderful!"

"What's come over her?" Angèle was taken aback.

Liza shrugged.

"She must have a fever. She said she had a headache."

Odette skipped in front of them.

"Yes, I have a fever. I've caught the flu!"

Liza grabbed her by the collar.

"Stop it. You look like a frog when you jump around like that."

"Well, you look like a pair of scissors when you run!"

"It's here on the right," said Angèle, turning off into a narrow alley that led to a grotto.

The grotto was cold and damp. Water dripped down the uneven stone walls.

"Now, line up, take each other's hands and close your eyes. Give me your hand, Odette. I'll lead. But you can't open your eyes until I say 'Open', and you can't say anything either. All right, let's go."

They shuffled forward uncertainly, treading on each other's toes and walking into one another as though they were blind.

"I'm scared," whispered Jacqueline.

Angèle squeezed her hand.

"Be quiet. It's right here. Be careful, there's a step."

Angèle stopped.

"Look now!" she announced loudly.

They opened their eyes. They were standing in a narrow corridor flooded with light. Tall glass walls rose up on either side of them, through which they could see enormous fish swimming languidly in clear green water.

Electric light filtered through the water, looking like pale moonlight.

"Snakes!" Odette grabbed at Liza's sleeve.

"They're eels, silly."

Shiny live black ribbons were slowly twisting and turning among the green seaweed.

"Oh, they're disgusting. Let's keep going."

They were quite alone. Their footsteps echoed hollowly.

"This is so strange. It's as if we're walking on the seabed," said Liza quietly. "Like the Jews who walked on the bottom of the Red Sea. There's water on either side."

Liza was standing next to Angèle, looking at the wall of water. The water looked green and cold, and it gurgled gently. Enormous fish swam heavily past them, slowly beating their fins as they went. They kept opening their mouths wide, while their flat round eyes stared blindly ahead. Liza imagined the glass cracking there and then. The water would come crashing down, and large, wet, slippery fish would swim across her, across her face and her breasts.

She shuddered.

"Look at that one!" Jacqueline laughed. "That one over there, the one lying on the bottom, with the red gills. Look at his face! He looks just like our history teacher. All he needs is some glasses."

Liza couldn't take her eyes off the fish. The gurgling green water, the pale light, their grotesque faces and glistening scales, the moist, heated air, all weighed on her like wearying moonlight.

Jacqueline's laughter seemed far, far away. Liza's knees grew weak. She wanted to lean against the glass wall behind which the fish were swimming. She wanted to stay there for ever. And she wanted Andrei by her side, not Jacqueline. She wanted him to be standing next to her, kissing her lips, while she observed the monstrous fish watching them. They would stand there for a long time, kissing, until they grew dizzy, and then they could lie down together on the damp earthen floor.

Liza turned to Odette.

"It must be nice to kiss here, in front of the fish."

"To kiss?" Jacqueline asked. "Do you kiss?"

Liza shook her head.

"No. But I would have kissed the dark boy from the film yesterday."

Jacqueline blushed.

"I'd hate to kiss a man. But I'd kiss you or Angèle…" She smiled dreamily. "This summer I was visiting my uncle in Brittany and I shared a bed with my cousin Simone. It was lovely. We always kissed when the moon was out."

"What does the moon have to do with it?" Angèle was surprised.

"When the moon was out, neither of us could sleep. And the moonlight made Simone look so pale and so delicate. Sometimes we'd spend the whole night kissing, until dawn."

"While the nightingale serenaded you in the garden?" said Georgette, laughing.

"No, the garden was full of frogs. They croak loudly all through the summer." Jacqueline paused for a moment. "But I couldn't kiss a man, it would be disgusting."

Liza shook her head.

"I don't understand. Odette and I have shared a bed lots of times, but we've never done anything like that."

Jacqueline blushed even deeper.

"Men are so coarse. And they don't shave properly. The stubble on their cheeks is always so prickly."

"But you don't even notice that when you're kissing them," said Odette quickly.

"How would you know?"

Odette lowered her gaze modestly.

"I'd just imagine that's how it is. Otherwise, nobody would ever kiss. Anyway, let's go. It's time to head home."

They made their way back to the street.

Angèle checked the wristwatch under her glove.

"We spent a whole twenty-five minutes on those fish! Last Thursday I went round the entire Louvre in forty minutes. And if I'd had proper shoes on, I could have done it in thirty."

Liza nodded to her friends.

"Goodbye then, I have to catch the tram." And with that, she scooped up her satchel and ran to the stop.

V

LIZA TOOK OUT her keys and unlocked the front door. The spacious hallway was dark and silent. She took off her coat and quietly tiptoed into the drawing room. The door to Natalia Vladimirovna's bedroom lay wide open, exposing the orphaned, empty space beyond.

"Has Natasha gone out?" Liza peered into the bedroom. The bed hadn't been made and the sheets were in disarray, hanging off it. A crumpled silk slip lay draped over the armchair.

The familiar smell of her perfume hung in the stale air.

"She's not here." Liza screwed up her face in disappointment and yawned. "I'm so dreadfully tired. And so dreadfully bored."

She went up to her room and laid out her textbooks and exercise book on the desk.

Nikolai's voice carried from the room next door:

"What an idiot! That Cromwell is such an idiot!"

"To hell with him." She heard Andrei's irritated reply.

"Andrei is here!" Liza fixed her hair in front of the mirror, smoothed down her short gingham dress and went through to her brother's room.

"You two are quiet. I didn't realize you were home!" Nikolai was smoking angrily.

"Oh, we're home all right. Where else can we go? We'll be at home from now on. All thanks to your Cromwell."

Liza sat down in the armchair by the window.

"Oh, Kolya, why are you so angry? It isn't his fault that he's run out of money. He took us out for two months in a row."

"And I developed a taste for it in those two months! I'm sick of sitting at home."

Andrei shrugged.

"I don't care. At least he's not going to be hanging around here now."

"Oh, give it a rest." Nikolai threw his cigarette on the floor.

Liza felt intensely bored.

"I'm going to go and do my homework."

"What's the hurry?" Nikolai looked at his sister mockingly. "It's not as if you're going out tonight."

Liza sat down at her desk and opened her algebra book. No matter how hard she tried, the problem wouldn't come out. Finally, she cracked it.

"There, I've figured you out, you stupid problem! You shouldn't have resisted. I said I'd solve you, and I did!"

"Dinner!" she heard Nikolai call from downstairs. She ran down.

A large light hung low over the table. Plates and glasses stood unsteadily atop a creased tablecloth. The knives and forks lay piled up in the middle.

"What service!" said Nikolai sarcastically. "It's no restaurant, is it?"

Liza sat down at the table and unfolded her napkin. The maid kicked the door open with her foot and walked in with a tureen full of soup. Liza dished out the soup for everyone before trying some.

"I don't like it."

"Just eat it, don't talk about it," Nikolai said. "You won't get anything nice here anyway."

Liza set her spoon to one side.

Andrei ate in silence, hunched over his bowl.

"We don't even have any beer in the house," complained Nikolai.

The meat was overcooked.

"Well, it's no Café de Paris," Nikolai said again. "That bloody Cromwell!"

"What's for dessert?"

"There's no dessert. *Madame* left only ten francs today. I don't even know how I managed to stretch dinner out of that, never mind dessert."

Liza drew her shoulder back irritably.

"Go back to the kitchen, Dasha."

"Perhaps you'd care for some tea? We have tea."

"All right, bring us some tea then."

Liza moved over to the divan.

"What on earth are we going to do now?"

"What are we going to do? Nothing." Nikolai shrugged. "You can sit around like a bobble head, nodding. And you can sing along to entertain yourself if you like:

> My head is nodding, nodding, nodding
> And my tongue is twisting, twisting, twisting...

There's nothing else to do."

Andrei stirred sugar into his tea.

"Of course, that isn't much fun."

Liza looked up.

"But why shouldn't we have some fun? Can't we go out and entertain ourselves? If we're bored with being at home, we can go to the boulevards and sit at a café."

"Not worth the candle. That'll cost you about fifteen francs, with the metro. Do you have fifteen francs, Liza?"

Liza shook her head.

"No."

"So put up or shut up." He paused. "That damned Cromwell. He's run out of money. He's pawned his own car. He says all that, but I remember him telling me that his mother keeps all her cash in an unlocked safe and that she can't even remember how many diamonds she owns!"

Liza looked at her brother.

"So? What of it?"

Nikolai said nothing. Liza looked at the mess on the table, at the leftovers on the plates, at Andrei's glowering angry face. The door to the drawing room was wide open. Trees were swaying noisily in the darkness outside.

Andrei yawned.

"It's a bore."

Liza yawned too.

"Yes, it's a bore. It's so boring that my nose hurts. Goodnight, I'm going to bed."

She got up.

"Come and say goodnight to me, Andrei."

Andrei placed a cushion under his head.

"I can't be bothered. I'm much too comfortable here."

"Up to you. Goodnight."

She walked through to the hallway and, without switching on the light, began climbing the staircase. A pale moon shone through the skylight. Black shadows of swaying branches ran up and down the white stairs. Liza gripped the banister and looked down at the hallway. It was silent and dark. A narrow sliver of yellow light streamed from underneath the drawing-room door. The large mirror on the wall glimmered duskily, like water— dark, silent, moonlit water, not with shadows, but with large, sleepy fish swimming in it, just like there had been at the fish museum. Liza suddenly felt an urge to have

Andrei with her again, to have him kiss her lips. To kiss and kiss until she grew dizzy.

"Andrei," she called out to him. "Andrei!"

"What? What do you want?" she heard him call out lazily in reply.

"Nothing. Nothing!" she shouted back. "Goodnight!" She paused to listen for his footsteps, but everything was still and silent. She let out a sigh and, feeling an uncomfortable lump in her throat that made it painful to breathe, slowly walked up to her room.

"Is this what love is?" she thought, locking her door. "Is life worth living if this is love?"

She undressed, removed the blue velvet cover from the divan and lay down, pulling the cover over herself.

The sooner she fell asleep, the better.

The divan felt too wide, wider than usual. The cold, heavy sheets weighed down on her breast. Maybe lying across it would be better, but she found it difficult to move. She lay still, pressing her cheek into the cold pillow.

Why was she so sad? Essentially, nothing had happened. Was it Andrei? Tomorrow he'll be kind and loving again. But what then?

Everything was fine. Everything was just splendid. Yet her anxiety was growing. What was it?

Wasn't she doing just fine? Didn't she have a fun life? She was so pretty and everyone was in love with her and she was the school's star pupil. What else was there? They were bored today because they had drunk too much the night before. Tomorrow they'd be having fun again. And everything was going to be all right.

But her heart was beating palpably and heavily. What was happening? Her blood was pumping slowly and heavily around her body. Her throat constricted with anxiety and fear. She opened her eyes. Dull moonlight was streaming in through the shutters. She looked at the desk, the textbooks, the uniform hanging up on the chair. It all looked so ordinary, just as it always did. It was dependable, familiar. "At school tomorrow, maybe I'll get called up to the front in the geography lesson." She forced herself to think of comforting childish things. "I'll go and play tennis with Odette."

But still her anxiety grew. The fear made her feet turn cold. What was happening to her?

The fear grew and grew. It was standing beside her, over her bed, pressing down on her chest until she could barely breathe. Then she heard a thin, shrill, piercing voice ring, like a mosquito, in her ear.

"The poor girl! The poor girl! What'll become of her? What's lying in store for her? She's asleep, she has no idea!"

With some difficulty, Liza managed to cast off the covers, grope for the light switch on the wall and turn on the light.

"What'll become of her?" she said. "Everything will be all right. I'll leave school and marry Andrei. But now I must sleep."

She switched the light back off and laid her head on the pillow again. But the fear and anxiety were still there!

"Sleep, sleep! I must sleep and tomorrow I'll wake up happy," she whispered.

She thought she felt the divan slowly creep upwards and dip back down again. "Like a rollercoaster," she thought. "I'm falling asleep, I must hurry." To hasten sleep, she pictured a flock of sheep on a riverbank. "Here I am taking one of them by the horns and leading it across the bridge. Here I am taking a second one by the horns…"

She felt uncomfortable. The air was stale and her hand pressed awkwardly into her cheek. But she mustn't move. She just had to wait until she fell asleep. Suddenly the river tilted and shot upwards like a mountain. The white rams started swimming rapidly through the green water. "Fish," Liza could just make out her thoughts. "I'm asleep," she whispered in blissful release.

VI

Bunny was sitting at a table in a restaurant, waiting for Natalia Vladimirovna. She had promised to be there at one, but it was already half past; Bunny was worried. He was just the same as always—he hadn't changed one bit, only now, instead of a cigar, he had a pipe, his bowler hat was dusty and a light summer coat replaced his long fur affair with the beaver collar.

In his pocket, Bunny had three hundred francs—three hundred francs that had been so difficult to obtain.

"One hundred francs for lunch and two hundred francs—for her."

It was all because of her. Because of Natasha. If only he could make her care! Oh, then everything would be very, very different. But she's heartless. She doesn't care. She doesn't take any notice. Seething with hatred, he stared at the chequered tablecloths, at the low square windows, at the walls daubed with lambs and piglets, at the whole faux-Normandy set-up. But his hatred wasn't really aimed at the restaurant. It was aimed at Natasha. He hated her. He hated himself, too. He hated her because she had ruined him and brought him to poverty and disgrace. "Poverty and disgrace"—those were his exact words. And he hated himself because he'd let himself be ruined.

A waiter carrying a menu came over to his table for the second time. Bunny waved him away in irritation.

"I'm waiting for a lady." He turned his head away.

But the waiter leant down to speak to him.

"Monsieur Rochlin, there's a telephone call for you."

"For me?"

Bunny leapt out of his seat.

"Where is your telephone? Where?"

Natasha's voice sounded through the receiver—loud and harsh.

"Hello, is that you? I can't join you for lunch."

"But… but why?"

"I can't."

He heard a click.

"Natalia Vladimirovna, Natasha!" Bunny cried out in a high-pitched voice.

There was no answer. He paused for a moment before dialling her number.

"*Madame* is not at home," the maid said. "*Madame* left an hour ago."

He threw down the receiver and raced back to his table. Without a word, he wrenched his coat from the stand, put on his dusty bowler at a tilt and bounded towards the exit, right past the startled waiter, who was looking at him reproachfully.

"I must find her!" The thought ran through his head.

VII

T HAT DAY, Liza returned from school early. There was nobody at home—no Natasha, no Kolya, no maid even.

Liza went through to her room and sat down on the light blue divan. Outside, wet auburn leaves spun silently down—like wet dead butterflies. The trees' thin, dark branches quivered pitifully. Rain hit the windows at an angle and ran down the panes in thin streams. The wet, shiny glass made this familiar scene appear strange—cruel and hopeless.

Liza sighed. How sad it was to sit in an empty house all alone. Even the street was empty. She was all alone. Like a castaway on a deserted island.

She reached out and plucked a book from the shelf. *The Devils*. She'd read it already. Oh well, it didn't matter.

She tucked her feet under herself and bent over the book.

'The Adventuress' was the chapter title. "It's when Shatov's wife comes back to him," she remembered. "I think it's a good one."

She read for a long time. Then she suddenly lifted her head.

"Nikolai Stavrogin is a scoundrel," she said out loud, and tears began to stream down her face. "Goodness, how beautiful! How can he write like that? How did I not realize this before?"

She clutched her hands to her chest. Everything had changed. Life had changed and she had changed. Life was beautiful and frightening, heartbreaking and poignant. And she, Liza, was now a grown woman, not the little girl she had been a moment ago. She was a grown woman who had shed tears for the first time—tears of pity, kindness and rapture.

"How beautiful!"

Liza got down on her knees and cried even harder, pressing her face against the silk upholstery of the armchair.

Her heart was breaking from gratitude, from too much love. Her head was full of confused, bewildering thoughts, and her hands were shaking.

"I have to do something. What though? I have to do something… not for myself—for others. I'll throw myself under a train, or walk into a tiger's cage. I must sacrifice myself and die. I must die."

She clasped her hands. "Yes, that's right. Not for myself—for others." She didn't want anything for herself, she just wanted others to be happy. She picked the book up off the floor and kissed it.

"Thank you, Dostoevsky, thank you!" she said aloud and wiped away her tears, so that she could carry on reading.

Amid the silence, she heard the click of a lock and the sound of rapid footsteps.

"Natasha's back."

She set the book down on the desk, ran downstairs and knocked on her mother's bedroom door.

"Let me in, Natasha."

"Later, Liza darling. I'm busy." Natalia Vladimirovna said in a rasping, hoarse voice.

What was the matter with her? Liza tiptoed to the dressing room. The glass door that led to the bedroom was covered by a heavy voile. Liza carefully drew the muslin aside.

Natalia Vladimirovna was sitting on the bed. A silver fox fur was draped over her shoulder. Her hat, shoes and gloves were lying in front of her on the rug.

Her face was not visible. She looked so sad. She must have been crying.

The fox's glass eyes were looking straight up at its owner. And with each passing moment, the fox looked sadder and sadder. Any second now it too would start to whine pitifully.

Natalia Vladimirovna turned her head. The light shone on her pale, miserable face. Tears were streaming from her large, painted eyes.

Liza stared at her in horror. Never before had her mother looked so pitiful, or felt so dear to her.

"Mama," she whispered in despair, as if she had only just realized that this beautiful, unhappy woman was her mother. "Mama."

She wanted to burst in and run to her mother, to console her.

She didn't yet know what she was going to say, but surely all her love and tenderness would be enough consolation.

Liza placed her hand on the doorknob, but just then someone rang at the front door.

"Dasha isn't here," she realized, and ran to open the door.

Solntseva was wearing a red waterproof cape. She walked straight in.

"Liza darling? Oh, this rain… Is Natasha at home?"

Liza looked at her with hostility.

"Yes, but I don't know if…"

But Solntseva wasn't listening. She quickly folded her umbrella and shook the raindrops off her hair, like a wet poodle.

"Is she in her bedroom?" she said, before marching on without waiting for an answer.

Liza watched in disbelief.

"Surely, she won't be allowed in, just as I wasn't."

Solntseva was already knocking on the door.

"It's me—Tanya."

The key turned almost immediately in the lock and a sobbing voice cried out: "I'm so glad you're here!"

Liza clenched her teeth bitterly.

"She shooed me away but she's happy to see her! I'm nobody to her."

She crept back to the dressing room, parted the voile and set about watching the goings-on in the bedroom.

Solntseva was now sitting on the bed, next to Natalia Vladimirovna.

"Calm down, calm down, Natasha."

Natalia Vladimirovna was sobbing on her friend's shoulder.

"He said to me, 'What would I want you for—you're old and have no money. Men don't love women like you.'"

"Now stop that, Natasha, don't mention him. Forget him."

"Forget him! How could I ever forget him! I love him. He's loathsome. He's stupid and nasty. He tells me to 'sling my hook'. Today he hit me… Right in the face."

Liza gasped and clasped her hands to her chest.

"He hit my mother! My mother!"

Her hatred for Boris and her pity for her mother caused the room to swim before her eyes and brought on a loud ringing in her ears. Liza clutched at the voile.

Meanwhile, Natalia Vladimirovna was speaking rapidly, her eyes flashing.

"I can't... I can't live without him."

Her hair fell over her face and she brushed it aside impatiently.

"He wants money. But where am I supposed to get it from? And it's never enough."

"You have to leave him, Natasha. Otherwise you're finished."

"Finished." She shook her head and her hair fell over her face again. "So be it. Let it be the end. I'm finished either with him or without him. I realized that today, when he hit me. You know, it made me love him more."

The doorbell rang again, quite suddenly and insistently.

"Surely, it can't be Boris! He wouldn't dare!"

Liza opened the door.

In front of her stood Bunny. Rain was streaming off his bowler straight onto his crumpled, sodden coat. Through the steamy lenses of his pince-nez, his eyes—round and blue, like porcelain—fixed her with an unhinged stare.

He moved his lips.

"Is Natasha... Natalia Vladimirovna at home?" he pronounced with some difficulty.

"Yes. But I think she's unwell. What are you doing still standing outside in the rain! Come in, I'll go and ask."

Bunny waved his hand dismissively and remained where he was.

"Call her. Tell her it's urgent."

"I will. But please come in. This rain… You'll catch a chill."

"Tell her it's urgent," he repeated and then closed his eyes as he leant his whole body against the rain-soaked wall, as if he were suddenly deathly tired.

Liza ran into the bedroom without knocking.

"Natasha, Bunny is out there in the rain. He's gone mad, he's scaring me."

Natalia Vladimirovna shrugged her shoulders in irritation.

"What does he want now? Go, send him away, Tanya. Tell him that I'm ill, that I have a fever."

Liza was now alone with her mother. She wanted to get on her knees, to kiss the small, naked feet that were swinging off the bed so helplessly, but she didn't dare. Instead, she silently held and stroked her mother's cold hand.

"What is it, Liza darling?" Natalia Vladimirovna asked absent-mindedly.

Liza wanted to reply, to tell her everything, but Solntseva was already walking back into the room.

"You must go to him. He's gone completely mad. He's just standing there in the rain. God only knows what he's capable of."

"Are you saying that I must go?"

"I'm afraid you must."

Natalia Vladimirovna obediently got to her feet, picked her hat up off the floor and put it on without even bothering to look in the mirror. Then she sat down in the chair and put on her stockings.

"He's in such a state. He gave me the fright of my life," Solntseva was saying.

Natalia Vladimirovna silently threw on her fur coat and tucked her hair under her hat.

"Goodbye, Tanya. Goodbye, Liza darling."

On the threshold she paused.

"Oh, how tired I am!"

Liza hugged her mother and, quite unexpectedly, surprising even herself, made the sign of the cross over her.

"What was that? What was that for?" Natalia Vladimirovna said with surprise, before walking through to the hallway and wrapping the coat around herself. "Happy now? Got what you needed?" she said, in quite a different, angry tone.

Bunny firmly held her by the arm, as if afraid that she would run away.

"The taxi is waiting."

She handed him her umbrella.

"Hold this."

They descended the wet steps into the wet garden. Bunny was carefully holding the umbrella in his out-stretched arm, slipping and sliding on the sodden earth, but all the while maintaining his balance like a tightrope walker. They climbed into the taxi.

"Don't sit so close to me. You're all wet."

Natalia Vladimirovna hid her face in her thick fur collar. Bunny was silent. They pulled up to a small hotel with a flashing sign. She raised an eyebrow.

"What on earth is this? Where have you taken me?"

"Let's go."

She shrugged her shoulders.

"Some sort of hideaway."

She waited with unconcealed disgust while Bunny made arrangements with the receptionist.

"Room twenty-five, on the third floor. The lift isn't working."

"That's the last thing I need! Oh, never mind. All I want is for this to be over."

She wrapped the coat more tightly around herself and quickly climbed the stairs. Bunny ran after her, breathing heavily.

On the landing he stopped to catch his breath.

"This is it."

The receptionist started briskly removing the piqué cover from the bed.

"No," Bunny waved his hand at him. "You may go."

The key clicked in the lock. Bunny turned to face Natalia Vladimirovna.

"Now," he said.

She stood before him in her black fur coat, looking tired and miserable. Stray strands of hair had fallen down from under her hat. She stared at him. The look in her eyes was malign and indifferent. A contemptuous smirk played on her pale unpainted lips.

"Now?" she said with disgust.

"Oh! She's unattractive… How could I have failed to realize this before?" The sudden thought crossed his mind. "This unattractive woman has caused me so much suffering, and now she'll be the end of me. She's unattractive." He wanted to hold on to this thought as if it were a lifebuoy. "She's unattractive and this means that I needn't have suffered and I needn't…"

He stared at her intensely, hungrily. She was unattractive and that meant that he was free. He could unlock the door and walk out and never think of her again. He was free, because she was unattractive.

"Well then?" she said. "Are we going to stand here in silence? Is this what you dragged me here for?"

The sound of her harsh, angry voice made Bunny's heart tremble in that familiar slavish way.

Free? No, he wasn't free. She might be unattractive, yes, but that didn't change anything. He had to go through with it. He remembered that he had made his mind up back at the restaurant. And now he had to go through with it.

With his stiff, disobedient fingers, he unbuttoned his coat and reached into his pocket.

"I'm going to kill you!" he screamed shrilly, pointing the revolver at her.

She didn't move a muscle. She stared at him in surprise, but there was no fear in her eyes.

"Go on, then. Kill me," she said quite quietly. "Kill me!"

She threw open her coat and lifted up her face, so he could take aim.

If she had been frightened, if she had stretched her arms out to him, if she had made a single step back, he would have fired. But she stood motionless.

"Practically point-blank," he thought dimly, "right into her heart. And then into mine."

But his hand was trembling and his fingers grew soft and weak.

He hung his head. The revolver fell to the floor with a thud.

"I can't," he said hoarsely.

"You can't? A pity…" She sank into a chair. The coat hung limply off her skinny shoulders. Her hands, still dressed in white gloves, rested wearily on her knees. They hadn't bothered to switch on the lights when they walked in, and now the room was very dark. She leant against the wall and closed her eyes. Her pale face was miserable.

"Natasha," he called out to her. "Natasha."

"What?" she said, without opening her eyes.

"Natasha, Natasha…" His shoulders trembled as tears streamed from under his pince-nez. "Forgive me. Forgive me, Natasha… I love you so much… Forgive me. I'm so unhappy…"

She stretched out a gloved hand.

"I'm not angry. I'm unhappy too…"

He didn't take her hand.

"No… No," he whispered, wiping away the tears with his hand. "No, wait. I don't want this. I want you to be happy."

She shook her head.

"How can I be happy?"

He hurriedly took out his chequebook. His tears obscured his vision.

"What am I doing?" The frightened thought occurred to him. "Oh, what does it matter! In an hour from now, I'll have shot myself."

He was already holding the pen.

"Twenty thousand. No, no, the whole thirty-five." He wiped his eyes and carefully wrote out the number on the cheque.

Now it was all over. He couldn't go on after this. This was the end.

She was still sitting there. It was as if she had forgotten all about him.

"Natasha," he called plaintively. "Natasha, here, take this."

She looked at the piece of paper glowing white in his hand, quite surprised. Then she took it and, leaning over it, studied it attentively.

Her white-gloved hands trembled. Her eyebrows rode up her forehead. In the dark, her eyes shone brightly.

"Bunny! Oh, my dear Bunny! Thank you! As it happens, I'm desperate for money."

Her voice rang out with happiness.

"Thank you, Bunny dear!"

She smiled at him and he fancied that he saw her pale, translucent face glow gently in the darkness.

He felt a pinprick to his heart. Quite unexpectedly, he remembered his childhood in Kovno and how a lit lamp would be brought through to the bedroom behind the watchmaker's shop. Not like the lamps these days, but a real kerosene lamp, with elegant, feminine curves—a beautiful lamp. And how a soft, magical glow would emanate through the matt white cover. And there was nothing on earth more beautiful than this lamp.

His whole body trembled.

"Natasha, I'm giving you my blood. I'm giving you my life, Natasha. Do you know where this money is from? It's someone else's money. It's the oil company's money," he whispered, afraid.

"Someone else's? Then take it back." She took the cheque out of her handbag. "Take it, tear it up."

"Keep it, keep it. It's yours, don't argue."

He peeled off his wet coat and threw his bowler down onto the table.

"Natasha, I want you to be happy. Smile again, please. Smile for me."

He got on his knees in front of her and slowly, with a painful tenderness, kissed her feet.

"Like a toad that's been tortured—pricked with pins all over—and that someone has finally given a drop of water to," she thought. And she closed her eyes in pity and disgust.

VIII

L IZA HAD BEEN LEFT standing in the hallway. She hadn't had time to speak to Mama. Never mind. It was actually better this way. She'd think everything over and then, when Mama came back…

"Mama, Mama, my Mama," she laughed out loud and ran into the drawing room. "My Mama." Not "Natasha", not "*her*" as Kolya and she would always refer to their mother. No. "*Mama.*"

Why shouldn't Liza be able to make her happy? Mama has no idea. She still thinks that Liza is a child. But Liza is a grown-up now and will sacrifice her life for Mama. That's right—her whole life. She just wants Mama to be happy.

Liza paced about the room excitedly.

"Boris. But he won't get in the way. He's stupid and unkind." She—Liza—would banish him.

At eleven, Nikolai arrived home.

"What are you doing here, Liza, curled up like an orphaned hedgehog? Go to bed."

Liza silently went upstairs to her room and lay down on the divan, covering herself with a shawl.

She had to wait up for Mama. Mama would be home soon.

But Natalia Vladimirovna still hadn't made it back by one o'clock. Liza fell asleep, fully dressed.

The next morning she awoke late, with a headache. As soon as she remembered the previous night, she ran downstairs. The maid was fussing about, irritably moving chairs around.

"Dasha, is Natalia Vladimirovna at home?"

The maid drew a sharp breath through her nose.

"Oh, she's home all right. But she's not alone."

Liza could barely breathe from anxiety.

"Who's with her? Bunny?"

"No, no. It's Boris... Boris Alexeyevich."

Dasha hunched her shoulders disdainfully, turned and set about dusting the sideboard.

"Is she awake?" Liza asked quietly.

"They've had coffee. And I've already been out to get him some ham."

She would have to wait. Liza sat down in her usual armchair in the drawing room.

She mustn't judge Mama. Poor Mama... She needed pity. Pity and love. Love from the bottom of her heart.

She could hear laughter from the bedroom. That hateful Boris was saying:

"Yes, that was a good call. A very good call. Well done you! I can depend on you!"

How strange. How everything had changed. Even yesterday morning, she had been utterly indifferent to Boris, whereas now she could strangle him with her bare hands. She stretched her arms out in front of her. This is how she'd strangle him. And she'd enjoy it too. The bedroom door flew open. Natalia Vladimirovna rushed into the drawing room, wearing a rose housecoat and treading with a new, light, happy gait. A smiling Boris followed her, the collar of his blazer turned up.

"Liza darling!" Natalia Vladimirovna cried gaily, embracing her daughter. "Have you heard the news? I'm leaving for Nice this evening."

"You're going to Nice?" Liza was shocked.

"Yes! Oh, I'm so happy! What a pity that I can't take you with us."

"You're leaving this evening?" Liza repeated. Her cheeks flushed and her eyes blinked again and again. "But what about me?"

Boris was studying her carefully with his bold black eyes.

"Like two cockroaches," thought Liza with disgust and turned away from him.

"Listen, Natasha," Boris said, while fixing his parting, "let's take her with us, she's such a pretty little thing!"

Slowly, he stretched out his arm, and slowly, he brushed her blonde hair.

"Charming! Still a child and yet—already a woman. Charming!"

Liza shook her head angrily.

"Oh!" He drew back his fingers and laughed. "A cub! She'll bite! Let's take her, Natasha, really. It'll be more fun."

Natalia Vladimirovna frowned.

"Stop it, Boris, Liza needs to study." She looked at her daughter coldly. "Why aren't you at school?"

Liza blushed again.

"I have a headache."

Natalia Vladimirovna felt her forehead.

"It's nothing. You don't have a fever. You should be ashamed of your laziness."

Upset, Liza bit her lip.

"I can still go."

"Of course you must go. You and Kolya shall see me off at the railway station this evening. Well, goodbye."

And she kissed her distractedly.

IX

IN THE HALLWAY, Liza put on her coat and picked up her satchel, which she had left there the previous day. She didn't have the right books, but it didn't matter. She just wanted to get out of the house as quickly as possible.

She walked down the street with her head hanging. Mama had never spoken to her like that before—coldly, almost hostilely. She had been hoping, dreaming... But now Mama was leaving that very evening. That meant that she wouldn't have time to explain. That meant that everything was lost.

Natalia Vladimirovna returned home just one hour before her departure. Liza rushed towards her.

"Oh, Liza darling, there is so much to do before I leave." She put down an armful of bags on the table. "Are my clothes packed? These must be packed, too. Help me, Liza darling, Dasha is utterly useless."

"I can help," said Boris.

Natalia Vladimirovna smiled at him lovingly.

"You? You can't help with anything, you'll only get in the way."

Liza was on her knees, kneeling over the wide-open suitcase. Natalia Vladimirovna was passing her bags and issuing instructions.

"Borya's yellow shoes can go at the bottom, they don't crease. Careful with the dress. You need to fold the blazer in half. It's so obvious that you've never been married!"

Boris sat in the chair, his legs outstretched. His feet almost touched Liza's shoes. His neatly coiffured head was inclined to one side; he was smoking and smiling.

"How could I have failed to notice that you have such a lovely little cousin? I've seen her countless times before, but never truly noticed her!"

Natalia Vladimirovna suddenly grew angry.

"Tuck your legs away, Boris. Am I supposed to keep jumping over them? Liza, you're going to crease everything like that. I'll do it myself. Go to your room."

"I've been really careful, I promise nothing will get creased. I'm almost done."

"No, go. I'll do it myself."

Liza got up.

"What about dinner?"

"We've eaten already. Go and get dressed, we'll be leaving for the station shortly. Is Kolya at home?"

"Yes."

"Call him down."

Liza left the room. She sat down on the stairs and rested her head on her lap.

"That's it. That's it. There wasn't time. It's all been for nothing. Now, I won't be able to say anything to her."

"Kolya," she called, without straying from her step. "Kolya, come down. Natasha is leaving." She quickly wiped her face with her hand. "I can't cry. If that horrible man sees, he'll laugh, and then Mama will be angry. Why is she getting angry? She never used to get angry."

Natalia Vladimirovna put on her travelling coat.

"Kolya, you're all grown-up now, and ever so clever." She stroked his head. "I'm going away for a month, so I'm leaving you money for housekeeping. Here, take it. Now, be sure not to lose it!"

Kolya carefully took the thousand-franc note, as if he'd never seen one before, folded it and stuffed it into his wallet.

"Be sure you don't lose it! And don't spend it all at once. I'm trusting you."

Nikolai kissed her hand ceremoniously.

"Thank you, Natasha."

"Now that you're in charge of the money, you're a grown-up. Are you proud?" She laughed. "Well, let's go. Liza, where are you?"

Dasha carried the suitcases out.

In the taxi, Natalia Vladimirovna sat next to Boris. Liza sat with Nikolai.

Nikolai was rubbing his hands with glee.

"Brilliant. We'll be able to live it up a bit on that! A thousand francs! We can get food on credit at the store later. Brilliant!"

Liza said nothing.

At the station there was a lot of fuss until the seats were finally located. When at last they settled down, Natasha Vladimirovna's face had lost the last traces of worry. It was as if everything she found sad and difficult were staying here in Paris, while ahead of her lay only happiness and sunshine. Natalia Vladimirovna smiled at them from the train window.

"Don't do anything silly. Study hard. Write to me often. I'll be back soon."

Boris peered out over her shoulder, sporting a travelling cap.

"They've put the heating right up. It'll be too hot to sleep."

Natalia Vladimirovna nodded happily, as if he were saying something incredibly pleasant.

"Yes, far too hot."

Then, still smiling, she leant out of the window.

"Give me your hand, Liza darling. May God keep you."

Liza grabbed hold of the thin hand in its white glove and pressed it against her lips.

"Mummy," she whispered, putting into that word all the words she hadn't had time to say.

Natalia Vladimirovna tore her hand out of Liza's grasp in a panic and quickly turned to look at Boris. But he was standing up in the car and hadn't heard anything.

"Never, ever say that! Remember that!"

The guard passed along, slamming all the carriage doors.

"Goodbye, Liza darling. Goodbye, Kolya." Natalia Vladimirovna's face was happy again. Next to her, Boris waved his cap at them, grinning and baring his white teeth.

Liza silently watched them pull away and then started running after the train, as fast as she could.

"Mama!" she shouted. "Mama!" She ran, colliding with other people on the platform, nearly knocking them off their feet. She couldn't see anything for her tears, nothing but the departing train. "Mama! Mama!"

Nikolai caught up with her and grabbed her arm.

"You're mad, you'll fall under the train! Why the theatrics?"

Liza stopped and wiped the tears from her eyes.

"Are you really that sad that she's gone? I'm not. I'm happy. We can have fun for a few days."

They made their way through the crowds towards the exit. Liza looked at the low, cold night sky and sighed.

"Let's get a cab, pick up Andrei and go somewhere. We'll drink to her departure."

Liza shook her head.

"I don't want to go anywhere. Take me home."

"You're being ridiculous, Liza. Funny and ridiculous. But please yourself. You can take the metro home—here's a franc."

X

THE WIND SWEPT noisily through the trees in the garden. The gate squeaked pitifully, like a cat.

Liza walked into the dark, quiet, empty house. She switched on the light and stopped by the coat stand, without taking off her coat.

It was all over. She didn't say anything, couldn't say anything. It was all over. What was she to do now? Do her homework, go to bed? What was the point in all that now? Now that it was all over. Mama had left.

She leant against the wall. She didn't cry. She looked listlessly at the white staircase, at the dark circular window and swaying branches outside.

She heard the heavy footfalls of somebody running up the porch stairs. The sound of the doorbell was desperately loud. Who could it be at such a late hour?

"Who is it?" she shouted through the door.

"It's me, Rochlin!"

"Bunny!"

The key clicked and the door opened. A cold wind

burst into the hallway. Bunny stood on the porch. Behind him the sky was darkening as the black trees swayed.

"Is Natasha, Natalia Vladimirovna at home?" he said breathlessly in his funny accent.

His blue round eyes stared at her in fright. He looked mad. His cheeks were tinged yellow and covered in stubble. His bowler hat was as crooked as could be without falling off. His coat was creased all over, his tie hung to one side. It looked as if he hadn't had a change of clothing for at least a day.

"Natalia Vladimirovna." He tugged at the collar that was too tight around his neck.

Liza stared at him—a funny man, mad, lost. She could hardly breathe for pity.

"Natasha isn't here," she said with difficulty.

"Where is she then?" His nose twitched, he seemed to be on the verge of tears. "I must, I absolutely must…"

Liza put her hand on his arm.

"Natasha's left," she said, as gently as she could.

"Left?" The mad blue eyes fixed Liza with a stare. "What, to go and sing at the restaurant?"

Liza shook her head.

"No, Bunny, she's a long way away… She's gone to Nice."

"Nice? Nice!?"

He jerked his head violently and his bowler hat came flying off, first hitting the wall and then rolling down the steps into the dark garden below. Bunny didn't even turn to look.

"Nice?" He repeated, shocked.

The wind ruffled the fine, soft hair on his head. His round face, with those mad eyes and his hair standing on end was both comical and frightening.

"Don't worry, Bunny." Liza pulled at his sleeve. "Let's go through to the drawing room, come," she said, as if there, in the drawing room, she would find the words to comfort him.

But he wouldn't move.

"She's left... She's left me... Tell me, Liza, did she go alone?"

Liza's heart thudded loudly and stopped.

"Yes."

"What about Boris? Was Boris at the station?"

Liza shook her head.

"I haven't seen him all week."

"She's left me." Bunny's shoulders shuddered. He hung his head and sobbed. "I gave her my blood and she..."

Liza embraced him urgently.

"Bunny, don't cry. Dearest Bunny, please don't cry. My fluffy, pretty little bunny. She's left me too, and I too am suffering. Oh, Bunny!"

They stood in the doorway, in the howling wind, embracing. Bunny put his short little arms around Liza's shoulders and pressed his wet cheek against hers, as if this little girl were his salvation, as if she alone connected him to life.

Liza kissed his wet, drooping cheeks. Poor man, he was so weak, so helpless! Her heart was bursting with pity, with tenderness, with dread. She just wanted to comfort him and help him. Poor, poor man.

Their tears mixed together. They held each other closely—both lonely, miserable, abandoned. "This is how people embraced on the *Titanic*, as it was sinking." The thought flashed through Bunny's mind. "And I am sinking. I have already sunk. It's all over."

"I wanted to die for her. I gave her my blood," he sobbed.

"Bunny, don't cry. Dearest Bunny, please don't cry. My little bunny. Natasha will be back in a month. We'll be happy yet, Bunny!"

He lifted his head. He even pushed Liza away a little. He took a crumpled handkerchief out of his pocket, blew his nose and wiped his face.

"Well, I should go. Thank you for taking pity on me." He smoothed down his coat, switching from tearful despair to his usual brisk manner. "Thank you, Liza dear. You're kind. Don't write or say anything about this to Natasha."

He let go of her hand and bounced down the stairs like a ball. Liza watched him crouch down and search for his bowler in the dark, find it, brush it off with his sleeve and replace it on his head, before bounding down to the garden gate. The gate creaked mournfully. Liza's heart was beating so fast, as if it wanted to burst out and fly after him. Poor, poor man. She wanted to comfort him, but how? She didn't know how, she couldn't help him.

She remained standing there in the doorway for a long time. She could no longer see anything or hear his footsteps. Everything was silent, dark and empty. There was only the sound of the trees and the dark sky. Liza shut the door and tried to warm her cold, stiff hands with her breath.

She wrapped herself in a shawl, sat down in her favourite armchair in the drawing room and sighed deeply.

"I'm unhappy and I'm crying, but what's my grief compared to Bunny's!"

She sighed again and tears streamed down her face.

"Poor wretched Bunny. Poor wretched Mama. Everyone is poor and wretched. Nobody understands anyone else, and nobody can comfort anyone. How difficult, how frightening life is."

Meanwhile, Bunny was walking down an empty, poorly lit street. His short coat was unbuttoned and his swollen lips gulped at the night air.

"This is the end. She's left me... like a mangy dog... Like a rabbit... It's all over."

In his head, everything was dark and confused. He didn't even feel any pain. It was the end.

But suddenly, somewhere deep in his subconscious, there was a bright spark, as if something had pricked his heart. A swooping gust of damp night wind struck him. He stopped. His knees began to tremble. A blissful weariness spread over his body, as if the cold light of the moon had replaced the blood in his veins. He heard a quiet, gentle ringing in his ears. He lifted his head and the ringing stopped. He looked at the sky. A cold, glistening moon slowly rolled out from behind a dark cloud.

"The moon," he whispered absent-mindedly and smiled.

And suddenly it all became clear—the blissful weariness, the trembling in his knees, the light of the moon streaming through his body.

"This is the end. She's left me... like a mangy dog." Suddenly, he understood that it really was the end. But not the sort of end that he had been anticipating, that he had been dreading. No. It was the end of his bondage, the end of his love. The end of his death. The death of his death.

He sighed in relief and touched his face.

"This is the end," he whispered gleefully. "I've made it. I've made it out alive. I'll live!"

He turned a corner. His step was light, he breathed easily and the trees rustled quietly, and up in the sky, the moon was swimming through dark clouds.

He took out his pipe and lit it.

"As for the oil company… I'll figure something out."

And he gave a dismissive wave of his little hand.

XI

THAT NIGHT, Liza couldn't get to sleep for a long time. Before bed, she said long prayers for her mother and for Bunny. She lay down on her wide divan and pulled the cover all the way up to her chin. On the wallpaper right above her pillow was a red carnation that reminded her of her mother's mouth. Liza lifted her head and pressed her mouth to the carnation with a passionate, loving tenderness.

"Mama, Mummy."

And again, she felt grief stirring in her chest. Not pity, but a living, breathing grief. Liza pressed her hand to her chest.

"Stop beating so. It will be over soon. Mama will come back. And I'll write to her. Yes, of course! Why didn't I think of this before! I'll write to her. I'll tell her everything in my letter."

She stretched out under the cover, laid her head back on the pillow and closed her eyes.

"I'll write, I'll write everything down."

A calm descended over her, she was almost happy. It wasn't over. Everything was going to be all right. Still smiling, Liza started composing the letter.

Dearest mummy, my darling mummy, you don't realize it yet, but I am an adult now, I'm not a child any more. And I love you more than anything in the world. I will sacrifice my whole life for you.

It was a long letter and Liza kept repeating it in her head.

"I'll forget it by tomorrow. Better write it all down now." She threw off the cover, switched on the light and sat down at her desk. She stayed in her nightdress, without putting anything over it. She tucked her cold, bare feet under her and dashed it off, trembling from joy, the cold and the excitement.

"I must have made lots of mistakes," she thought, worried. "Writing in Russian is so difficult. But Russian is better—it's more tender. Mama will forgive me." She folded the sheets of paper and placed them in an envelope, without bothering to reread them.

"I'll send it as soon as I get Mama's address." She jumped back into bed and kissed the red carnation on the wallpaper.

"Goodnight, Mummy. You're on the train right now. You don't know it yet, but soon you'll get this letter." Then she pulled up the cover and fell immediately asleep.

Three days later, a postcard arrived.

My dear Liza, it's wonderful here and I'm having lots of fun.
What a pity that you aren't here! Hugs and kisses to you and
Kolya. Write to me at…

On the other side, across the sky and the sea, she read:
"For God's sake, don't forget to address me as Natasha in your
letters!" Natasha was underlined.

Liza read the postcard and twirled it in her hands.
Then she unlocked her bureau, took out her letter and
tore it into tiny little pieces. That letter had been written for Mama. Whereas Natasha could make do with a
postcard in a day or two.

Liza ran downstairs. Nikolai was drinking coffee in
the dining room.

"Look who's written."

Nikolai snorted with disdain.

"Is she having fun? Well, let her. We don't miss her
either. She could have left a little more money though."

Liza nodded.

From that day on, she stopped thinking of her mother
and even avoided going into her bedroom.

Part Three

I

THAT WINTER in Paris—the winter of '28—was bitterly cold. In the mornings, the frozen earth of the garden would creak under Liza's feet.

Liza went to school. School was boring. Home was even more boring. It was as if she were living on her own. Nikolai would disappear for days on end, returning only late at night when she was already asleep. He and Andrei were always whispering about something and had stopped inviting her out with them. But Liza did not even care to go to restaurants. She felt weak, tired and indifferent to everything. She just wanted to sit by the fire with a book. Even Odette was away—she was with her grandmother in Bordeaux. But Liza didn't give any thought to Odette.

Liza was on her way home from school. Her satchel weighed her arm down. Her legs were cold in her thin stockings.

"It's nothing." She lifted up the collar of her light jacket—the one with gold buttons—and pulled her beret down a little farther. "Don't pay any attention to it."

She saw a white round piece of cardboard lying on the pavement in front of her. She picked it up and threw it with all her might. It flew high up into the clear, frosty air. "Like a white dove," she thought and turned around.

Andrei was walking straight towards her.

Liza was happy.

"Hello! Have you come straight from school?" she asked.

"I've stopped going."

"Why?"

"I couldn't be bothered any more." He shrugged his shoulders. "Nikolai's stopped going too."

"That's not good," Liza said quite seriously. "What's going to happen now? They'll make you retake the year or expel you."

"So what? What do we care about the future?"

"Does your aunt know?"

"No, she doesn't."

Liza shivered.

"It's so cold. Do you want to run? It isn't far. Give me your hand."

Andrei ran too fast. Liza couldn't keep up with him. He was dragging her by the hand and she kept tripping.

"Let go! Let go! I can't!"

He pushed open the gate.

"It's so slippery, I'm going to fall over!"

But they were already at the porch.

"What fun!" Liza walked into the hallway and threw down her satchel and coat on a chair. "Let's go to my room, quick, and light the fire."

As he was taking his coat off, she stood up on tiptoe and kissed him.

"Your ears are so cold. Kissing you is like eating ice cream. I'm so glad I ran into you. We haven't been alone together for so long."

She looked into his eyes.

"You're practically a stranger these days."

He shook his head.

"No, Liza."

She no longer felt happy. She picked up her books.

"You're all I have," she said quietly, blushing. She hurried on.

Firewood was stacked up next to the fireplace in her room.

Liza sat down on the rug.

"Come on then, help me. We need some heat in here."

Andrei got down on his knees beside her.

"Wait, don't just throw the logs on like that, the paper goes first."

He struck a match. Liza couldn't pull her eyes away.

"I like fire. Put some more logs on, come on."

"That's enough, let them catch. It'll be warm soon."

She started piling more logs on. Her eyes were wide with excitement. Her cheeks flushed scarlet.

"That's enough, that's enough!"

She wasn't listening to him, she was throwing more and more logs on.

"Like a bonfire." She was staring into the flames. "You know, I want to be burnt alive. Kolya always says that if I had been alive in the Middle Ages, I should have been burnt at the stake, like a witch."

"Oh no, you would have been a nun, with those eyes of yours. Or maybe a nun and a witch in one."

Liza clapped her hands.

"That would have been wonderful! All day I would pray and eat nothing, wear a black dress and a cross and kneel. And at night I would fly on my broomstick to a witches' Sabbath." She straddled the fire poker. "Haw! Haw! I fly up and down and my feet don't touch the ground!" she shouted loudly. The red glow of the fire lit up her face.

Andrei shuddered.

"Stop it, you're too much like the real thing."

She laughed again and threw more logs onto the fire.

"You know," he said, "if this is what you're like, you should write poetry."

Liza shook her head.

"I don't want to. Only the stupid and the old write poetry these days."

"You're a funny one, Liza. What does it matter what it was like before compared to these days? What would you have us do now?"

Liza lifted her face to his.

"Now, we have to live and not dream about anything."

He looked at her pale face, at her bright limpid eyes.

"You must find that hard."

"Well, irrespective of whether it's hard or not, it's what we must do." She shrugged. "It's too hot. Let's go and sit on the divan."

Andrei sat down next to her. They were silent.

"It gets dark so quickly. No, don't turn the light on, Andrei. It's nicer like this."

The logs crackled in the fireplace. The red light of the fire fell on the divan, on Liza. She reached her hands out towards the flames.

"You know, Andrei, I keep thinking," she said slowly. "I keep thinking how difficult and dreary life must be if childhood is as good as it gets. And if it's all downhill from here, I don't want to grow up." She shook her head. "And, you know, I don't think I ever will."

"Nonsense, Liza. It's only because you're fourteen. Fourteen is the worst age. You'll be fifteen in March and it will all be much easier then."

She shook her head again.

"Oh, no, no. I don't believe that. It won't get any easier, or any better."

He didn't reply.

"Why are you so sad, Andrei?"

"I'm not sad at all."

"Yes, you are. Don't argue. You're always sad. Right now you look terribly like a sad bird of prey. Like a falcon." She took his hand. "'*Et alors, parce qu'il était toujours triste, on l'appela Tristan,*'" she said slowly and sighed. "Why did you stop loving me, Andrei?"

He kissed the palm of her hand.

"I love you, Liza."

"That's not true. You never visit me. You spend all your time with Kolya."

"We have things to do."

"What sort of things?"

He leant towards her.

"I love you, Liza. Trust me. I'm not to blame. It's very difficult for me. I'm sick of it all."

She enfolded him in her arms.

"If you love me, then I don't need anything else. It's difficult for you and it's difficult for me, too. But it's a little easier when we're together."

He laid his head on her lap.

"Forgive me."

"There's nothing to forgive. It happens all the time. Even when you really love someone, you can forget all about them for a while. Like Tristan and Isolde. Do you remember?" She stroked his hair. "In Biarritz, I barely thought of you."

He raised his head from her lap.

"You forgot all about me then. Because of Cromwell?"

She placed her hand on his forehead.

"Lie back down. It doesn't matter why, because I love you again now."

He clenched his fists.

"I hate him."

She leant down towards him.

"Your face is so angry. Don't be jealous. It was all so long ago."

She kissed him.

"It's so nice being with you. If only we were together always."

"We'll always be together, Liza."

"I don't believe that. How dark it is."

"Hold on, let me tend the fire, or else it'll go out."

She held him.

"Don't."

The fire suddenly flared up, flames darted this way and that, and then it went out. It was completely dark, blissful and silent. Andrei kissed her knees in the dark. Her lips sought out his.

"Is that you, Andrei? Do you love me?"

She sighed quietly and closed her eyes.

"Oh, no, no. It would be too perfect. It can't be, it never is. You won't come to see me tomorrow."

Somebody was climbing the stairs. The door flew open, the light switch clicked.

Liza scrunched up her eyes against the light and

hurriedly pulled her skirt over her bare knees. Nikolai walked in.

"What are you two doing sitting around in the dark, like a pair of moles?"

Andrei got up and fixed his tie.

"Didn't anyone teach you to knock?"

"Come off it! Liza's my sister, isn't she? Do what you like, you two. I couldn't care less."

He sat down on the divan and lit a cigarette.

"We can't go on like this. We have to get our hands on some more money, no matter what."

Liza walked over to the mirror and smoothed down her ruffled hair.

"Yes, yes, we've heard it all before. You're like a broken record."

I I

LIZA WAS RIGHT—Andrei didn't come the next day. She waited for him in vain. But by the evening, she was quite calm. What of it? He could do as he pleased. She should just stop thinking about him, and that would be the end of it. And so everything returned to normal—only she felt that little bit sadder.

It was Christmas Eve. Liza was sitting in her room, on her own. A light drizzle drummed steadily on the roof. A car, gleaming from the rain, was driving slowly down the road. A beaming young woman glanced out of its window. All the seats were covered with shopping bags.

"It's Christmas Eve," thought Liza. "Everyone's out buying presents and having fun." She could just picture the bustling streets—a sea of wet umbrellas, and crowded shops full of women—exhausted shoppers demanding things from exhausted shop assistants, like one great cheerful hell.

"And later tonight they'll switch on the Christmas tree lights and have a gay old time. Am I just going to sit here by myself all night?" She shook her head. "No, no, I'm going to go out to the cinema," she decided. "It's nice there. I can get some roasted chestnuts on the way. It'll be warm there, and I'll be able to think about something else. I can have fun on Christmas Eve, too!"

She ran downstairs.

"What about you? Would you be brave enough?" She heard Nikolai's loud, forceful whisper. "Could you do it? Or would you lose your nerve?"

"I'm no coward," Andrei answered resolutely, angrily.

"What on earth can they be talking about?" Liza opened the door.

Nikolai gave a startled jump and turned around to face her.

"Who's there?" He was very pale. Andrei stood smoking by the window. Nikolai studied his sister with suspicion.

"What do you want?"

"I'm going to the cinema. I need twelve francs."

Nikolai spread his arms wide and gave a low whistle.

"Twelve francs? Have you been living under a rock? Haven't you noticed we've not had a centime in this house for three days straight?"

Liza shrugged.

"That's a pity."

"Oh, please, don't give me that. You sound like some affronted princess! You could've gone to the cinema when we had money. So don't start complaining now. I'm sick enough of it all as it is."

"It's Christmas Eve," Liza reminded him.

"And? What does that matter? Leave us alone, we have things to discuss."

Liza went back up to her room.

"Oh, what a bore, what a bore, what a bore." She yawned loudly.

She didn't even have anything to read; she'd read all the books from cover to cover, several times over.

She caught a reflection of herself in the mirror above the fireplace. Her face looked pale and drawn.

"Goodness, I look so miserable. That's how I'll look when I'm lying in my coffin."

She crossed her arms across her breast. All she had to do now was close her eyes.

She shook her head and her fair hair fell over her face.

"It's Christmas Eve and I'm thinking about death. That's no good."

She looked out of the window. It was Christmas time, but it didn't look like it. The rain was still drumming on the windowpanes. Tired, wet trees were bending in the wind. The street was empty. Through the veil of rain and the screen of water running down the windowpanes, everything looked vague and elusive. Of course, none of it was real. It was only there *pour rire*. She wasn't actually real either. And all her life was actually *pour rire*, too—just for a laugh. Although it wasn't at all funny.

She turned away from the window. Oh, the slush! Christmas was supposed to be ice-cold and snowy, like in Moscow. *Moscow*. She drew up her knees and leant into the cushion.

Moscow. She closed her eyes and tried to picture it in her mind's eye. Snow, snow, snow. White, light and bright. It made everything white and sparkling. Snow on the ground, snow on the rooftops, snow floating in the air. She remembered that much, but other than that… other than that it was all a muddle. She could picture Moscow quite clearly, the Moscow of her childhood, but that wasn't the real Moscow either. Wide boulevards blanketed in snow, the Kremlin, and next to it—a tall yellow Chinese pagoda. Slightly farther off—a garden, and palm trees laden with coconuts. Under the palm trees stand bamboo huts and a grey five-storey building. In a pond are ships, goldfish, swans and crocodiles. The streets are filled with crawling trams, flying horse-drawn sleighs and sprinting long-legged ostriches. The pavements are bustling with people dressed in fur coats and fur hats—officers and ladies—and also strolling Indians with feathers in their headdresses and naked Negroes riding giraffes. And over by Kuznetsky Bridge, down on the ice, lives a white polar bear, and the sky sparkles pink all night long with the dancing Northern Lights.

That's the Moscow Liza remembers. Moscow filled with tigers, torpedo boats and parrots from her father's stories, gathered on his travels. Liza's father had been a naval officer. She loved him more than anything, but he kept going off to war. One spring there had been a lot of shouting in the street, right under their windows. Mama (that was Natasha's name back then) said that it was a revolution. Mama looked very frightened and Liza started crying. And then there came a letter. It was delivered in the morning, while they were drinking tea. Mama read it and fell to the floor—and her teacup fell, too, and smashed into pieces. When Mama got up, she said that the sailors had drowned Papa in the sea and that he was up in heaven now. Liza couldn't understand how Papa could be up in heaven if he was in the sea. Unless he'd turned into a flying fish? Then he'd be able to live both in the sea and up in heaven.

It was when they arrived in Constantinople that Liza realized that Papa lived far, far away on the horizon, where the sea met the sky. Liza spent day after day lying on top of a dusty suitcase in a dark corridor of their hotel. Directly above the suitcase was a small window, with a small patch of sea and a small patch of sky. In the evenings, a star would light up in the small patch of sky, and the small patch of sea would grow dark and restless.

Liza gazed through the window all day long. That's where Papa lived, where the sea met the sky. Perhaps he would swim over to see Liza, just for a minute? Surely, he hadn't forgotten her? She didn't tell anyone about this, not even Kolya. And on the rare occasions when she was taken to the beach, she'd secretly throw crumbs into the water for Papa.

Mama (she was still "Mama" then) worked in a restaurant. She used to cry, "I can't do this any more, I'm so tired. My feet ache." Liza would sit down on the floor in front of her and stroke her feet. How could such beautiful feet cause so much pain? Kolya used to kiss Mama. Mama would embrace them both. "My poor little orphans. I wouldn't put myself through this if it weren't for you. I'd just lie down and die."

Two years later Liza understood that Papa was dead and felt ashamed when she recalled the flying fish. She felt those thoughts must have been sinful. She never told anyone about the flying fish.

They moved to Paris. Mama began working as an assistant in a shop. And that's when it all happened. All of a sudden she became happy again and was singing all the time. One night, when Liza was nine and Kolya was twelve, when they were already at school, Mama told them to never call her "Mama" again, and to call her Natasha instead. She said that all their troubles were over. She said that she'd run into her cousin once removed, Uncle Sasha, who was very rich.

Nobody had heard anything about Uncle Sasha before. But the very next day he appeared—a fat, dark Armenian with a large diamond ring on his finger. They moved out of their single hotel room and into an apartment in Passy. Kolya was sent to boarding school—he was disrespectful to Uncle Sasha. Liza cried a lot when that happened. That summer, they went to Trouville.

Without bothering to open her eyes, Liza plumped up the cushion under her head.

Trouville. Trouville, she remembered it well.

…The tide was out. The sea had retreated to reveal a wide white sandbank. A rowing boat bobbed up and down on the grey waves. A fisherman in a red jacket sat in it. An ashen pink sun hung high in the grey sky.

Liza waded ankle-deep into the water. A fat green crab gingerly picked its way between the seashells. Liza bent over it and flipped it onto its back. The crab started waving its claws around frantically, trying to bury itself in the sand.

He was so big! Should she take him to their pension and have it cooked for dinner? She shrugged. There wasn't any need for that, they were hardly going to starve. She picked up the crab and threw it back into the water. "Go home, silly, go and live another day…" She had been there almost a month, but she still wasn't used to it all. She sighed and looked out into the distance. How strange the sea looked, and the sky. It was all so pale and misty. Even the sun, too. And the breeze—it was like nothing else, so light, humid and barely palpable. And the sand was grey. Never had she imagined that such a place existed.

It was like living in a dream.

Natasha was sitting by an orange-and-white tent, reading a French novella. Liza quietly walked over and sat down beside her.

"Natasha, tell me about Moscow."

Natasha looked up at her absent-mindedly.

"Go and play, Liza."

"I'm bored."

"Go and catch some crabs."

Liza shook her head.

"I don't want to. I read that in Russia people go out to pick mushrooms. That must be fun!"

"Nonsense. Catching crabs is much more fun. Go and play with the children. Stop disturbing me."

Liza got up obediently and left.

A boy was pulling a toy ship along on a string.

"Are you the captain?" Liza asked him.

"I am. I have gold buttons, see?"

"So why aren't you sailing on your ship?"

"Nonsense. It would sink with me on it."

Liza nodded.

"Precisely. You could go down with your ship."

The boy turned away from her angrily.

After that, some of the children started building a sandcastle. Liza stood and watched them for a while. What was the point of going to all that effort when the tide would wash it all away anyway? Liza ran back to her mother.

"Natasha, what's the best way to get to the Kremlin from Tverskaya?"

"What?"

"What's the best way to get to the Kremlin?"

"Oh, you're on about Moscow again." Natasha smoothed out her skirt over her naked legs. "I don't remember. You can find out for yourself when you go to Moscow. Stop disturbing me now."

Liza squinted her eyes and looked out over the pale waves.

"Natasha, can I go for a swim?"

"You've been in the water already this morning. It's bad for you to go in twice."

"Please, Mama! It's so hot. Please!"

Natasha frowned indolently.

"Very well. You can go in, but be careful."

In the tent, Liza quickly undresses and pulls on her yellow bathing costume. It's still damp.

She runs across the wide sandbank. Faster, faster! The water is so warm. Liza throws up her arms and dives in. She's swimming. The waves are so wonderful. It's lovely.

She turns over to swim on her back. Of course, like this she could last around six hours, perhaps even longer.

The fisherman in the red jacket is now wading waist-deep in the water, watching the swimmers.

"You swim like a fish," he tells her.

She blushes with delight.

"I'm training."

"Training for what? Are you planning on swimming across the Channel?"

"No. I'm doing it just in case."

She dives down, then resurfaces and shakes the water from her hair.

"In case of what?" He sounds surprised.

"In case of a shipwreck," she says earnestly, before swimming off.

They have dinner at a table of their own.

"Liza, take your elbows off the table."

Uncle Sasha and Natasha are arguing quietly, as usual.

"So, you're going to the casino again?" Uncle Sasha is asking her.

"Why wouldn't I?"

"Because I'm asking you not to."

Natasha's grey eyes well up with tears. Uncle Sasha angrily moves the mustard pot across the table.

"Here we go again. You're so unhappy. You're such a victim. We're leaving the day after tomorrow, you could at least…"

Liza drops her fork on the floor.

"As soon as that!"

Uncle Sasha turns to look at her.

"Manners, Liza. You're a big girl now."

Through the window she can see white roses, green grass and a pale sky.

They finish their dinner in silence. Liza removes the fresh figs from her plate and quickly stuffs them into her pocket.

Liza slowly makes her way along the sandy alley. She bends down to smell the gillyflowers. She's just taking a walk before bedtime, nothing to it. All she's thinking about is the garden, the gillyflowers and the roses.

But the moment she draws abreast of a tall fir tree, she turns around to check whether anyone is watching her. Then she runs into the white summerhouse and slams the door behind her.

Nobody has spotted her. She squats, lifts up one of the floorboards and gropes around in the dark recess below.

Nobody's taken it. It's still all there. She takes out a bundle wrapped in a handkerchief and empties it out onto the table. She counts out the money. Fourteen francs, thirty centimes. It isn't much, but she can't wait any longer. They're going back to Paris the day after tomorrow. And she could just be really careful with her spending… Also in the bundle are nuts, a few figs and a bar of chocolate. Nuts are very nutritious. If she has two nuts and a fig a day, she's got enough to last her twelve days. And then there's the chocolate too.

She ties the bundle back up and returns it to its hiding place. It's safer there. It could well get discovered at home. Still squatting, she takes out an envelope from the folds of her dress. The envelope contains a postcard with a view of the Kremlin and, most importantly, a page she had torn from a book.

Liza studies the postcard. At least she can be sure that she'll be able to recognize the Kremlin. Then she unfolds the page and starts reading:

Robert stealthily joined a group of porters at the harbour. They were carrying heavy sacks. He climbed a rope ladder up the side of the ship and made his way to the hold without anyone noticing. The loud clanking of chains and the crew's shouting brought him the welcome news that the ship had finally got under way. In the corner of the hold he spotted a bundle of tarred ropes and was about to make himself comfortable on them, in anticipation of the long journey ahead, when suddenly the door flew open with a loud creak. Two hulking sailors stood in the doorway. Robert's heart stopped in horror and the hair on his head stood on end.

"There's someone in here," said one of the sailors, as Robert felt a strong hand grab him by the collar.

"Take him to the captain," said the other, and soon, after a few energetic kicks from the sailors, Robert found himself before the captain. The captain spat his chewing tobacco over the side of the ship, swore masterfully and said to Robert:

"Who are you? And what are you doing here? I'm warning you, speak only the truth or you'll find yourself feeding the sharks at the bottom of the sea." And with that he pointed his tanned brown hand towards the blue waves and the monsters' faces among them.

"I am Robert de Costa Rica," Robert declared, his voice as clear as a bell. "I'm trying to reach Spain, my long-suffering homeland, which has been enslaved by the Moors. With sword and cross I shall conquer its enemies."

"You are a fine young man," said the captain, slapping his shoulder. "You may stay with us. But, pray, what skills do you have?"

"I can do anything you say, Captain."

"Very well." The captain threw him a brush. "You can scrub the deck."

Liza had read this page so many times that she knew it by heart.

It contained everything she needed to know—the rest was easy. She could walk to Le Havre from here. If she left at dawn, she would make it by nightfall. At Le Havre she would find a ship bound for Russia.

She squeezed her eyes shut. She could see herself at the harbour, surreptitiously joining a group of porters. She could see herself climbing the rope ladder up the side of the ship and then sitting in the hold on top of the tarred ropes. Chains rumble. The ship gets under way. The captain looks at her. "Who are you and what are you doing here?"—"I'm Russian and I'm going to suffer for Russia." She's given a brush and she scrubs the deck.

To suffer for Russia.

It's Easter. Kolya is home for the holidays. The walls of the nursery are covered in colourful wallpaper. From the window they can see the Bois de Boulogne. They're playing "Kooksa and Krooksa". Kolya is Kooksa and Liza is Krooksa. Krooksa is paying Kooksa a visit and Kooksa is fussing over her kindly. "Krooksa darling, please make yourself comfortable in the coal box, you'll be ever so cosy in there. If you're cold, you can open the umbrella." The nursery door is open and they can hear their nanny in the dining room, preaching to Dasha the maid.

"It's for those sins. For all those sins. Just look at *madame*, she's come here and given Russia up. She's forgotten all about her motherland! She's hauling herself round theatres and restaurants, waiting to have Russia handed back to her on a platter. Oh, no, you don't! You have to suffer for Russia. Suffer!"

Liza shudders. A chill rolls down her neck and between her shoulder blades, like a cold marble.

"You have to suffer!" Nanny's voice drones on.

Kolya shakes Liza by the arm.

"Why don't you say something, Krooksa dear? Would you like a spoonful of boot polish or not?"

Liza gets up from the floor and brushes the sand off her dress. That's right, she must suffer. That's why she's going to Russia. To suffer. For all of them. To suffer for beautiful Natasha who's having too much fun to even remember how to get to the Kremlin from Tverskaya. And most importantly—to suffer for Russia.

Liza lifts her head up high, crosses her hands over her chest, just like Christian martyrs in paintings, and makes her way back across the garden, slowly and solemnly.

In Natasha's room, the shutters are closed and the electric light is on.

Natasha is sitting in front of the mirror in a sparkling pink dress, carefully powdering her shoulders.

Uncle Sasha is standing behind her in a dinner jacket, adjusting his black tie.

Liza stops to admire them. This is her Mama. So pretty and so glamorous! And this is the last time she's going to see her.

"Natasha!" She runs to her mother with her arms outstretched. "Natasha!"

Natasha holds her back.

"Calm down, calm down. That's quite enough of that."

She takes a step back. Liza looks at her beautiful legs in their pink silk stockings and her gold shoes with their shiny buckles.

"Give me a kiss, Natasha!"

Natasha leans over her and carefully, so as not to smudge her lipstick, gives her a kiss on the cheek.

Liza inhales the heavy, familiar scent of her perfume.

"Again, again!"

"Stop it, Liza dear." Natasha is annoyed. "You've tired yourself out again. Go to bed at once."

Liza walks over to Uncle Sasha.

"Goodnight."

He pats her head gently.

"You're so pale and thin! You've only got your eyes left! Should we have brought you here? You've got even thinner, if I'm not much mistaken…"

The door closes behind them. She's never going to see them again. They'll still be asleep when she leaves tomorrow.

Liza feels hurt and upset. From the wardrobe, she takes out her yellow shoes with the thick soles, clean linens and a waterproof overcoat. That's everything. Now she can go to bed.

She turns off the light and stretches out under the duvet. She must get to sleep quickly. Tomorrow she'll have to get up at the crack of dawn. But she feels so hurt and so upset. Mama didn't even turn to look at her—she only saw her through the mirror.

Moonlight is streaming in through the open window. A thin silver line shimmers across the floor. The polished wardrobe glimmers dimly. The linens show bright white against the armchair. Slender branches sway in front of the windowpanes, as dark clouds swim across the sky. It is so sad, so quiet.

Liza turns to the wall and presses her eyes shut. "Mama. No, I mustn't think of Mama, or else I won't be able to get to sleep." It would be better to go over everything again—she's at the harbour, she joins a group of porters, the rope ladder, the hold.

So quiet. So sad.

"The hold." She lets out a sigh in her sleep. "What comes next? Oh, that's it, the ropes." "You're a fine girl!" The captain's voice booms. "Take this brush and scrub the deck."

Liza opens her eyes in alarm. It's already light. A fresh chill drifts in through the window. The clock strikes five.

The grass glistens with the morning dew. The sky is a pale grey, almost white. Liza is walking down a wide road. She's done it. Nobody even noticed. It's so easy to walk, so easy to breathe. But she mustn't hurry or she'll tire herself out. She takes long, measured strides in her yellow shoes and swings her arms in time to her walking. That's how real hikers walk.

It begins to get hot. She removes her hat and wipes the sweat off her brow. She looks up at the sun. It must be one already.

They'll be having lunch in the pension. Mama will have noticed that she's missing. She's looking for her, worried. Mama. No, she mustn't think of Mama.

Motor cars race past her. Liza chokes on the dust and rubs her eyes. She's tired. The waterproof coat weighs her arms down. She has a headache. If only she could lie in the shade under the trees and sleep. But then she'd feel even wearier.

Soldiers always sing when they're marching some-where. It's easier to walk with a tune. She doesn't know any soldiers' songs. She doesn't know any songs at all, in fact. Except for the one about the little animal. It's a stupid song, but that doesn't matter.

She starts singing, trying to keep the pace.

> Once upon a time
> There was a little beast
> He hopped along a path,
> But was neither frog nor ferret.
> Whoever would have thought it?

The wind blowing dust into her face makes it difficult to sing. Her yellow shoes are rubbing.

"Who would have ever thought it?"

A peasant cart rattles past her. A suntanned old man is sitting tall in the driver's seat. Beside him sits an old woman in a red woollen dress. Gosh, it's the dairymaid! Liza quickly turns her face away. The road is straight, surrounded by open fields. There's nowhere to hide.

"Look there," she hears the dairymaid say. "Isn't that the Russian girl from the Excelsior? They said she's gone missing."

"Nonsense," she hears the man's voice reply. "She couldn't have walked all this way."

Her knees grow weak from fear and her sight grows dim.

"I'm telling you, that's her."

Liza tries to outstrip the cart.

"Hey, hey, you!" the dairymaid shouts.

Liza is almost running.

"Hold the horses, we've got to check."

The dairymaid jumps off the cart and lands with a thud.

Liza makes a dash for the nearest field.

"Stop! Stop!" the dairymaid calls after her.

She's so close. Liza can hear her clogs thudding against the ground and tries to run faster, gasping for breath.

The old woman grabs her by the shoulder and looks her straight in the face.

"I knew it. It's her, all right!"

"Leave me alone!" Liza tries to fight her off. "You don't have any right to stop me. Leave me alone!"

But the old woman drags her over to the cart.

"You're a wolf cub, you!" She shakes Liza by the shoulder, angrily. "You bit me and drew blood! I'm not letting you go now."

She lifts Liza up and hoists her onto a sack of potatoes.

"Keep an eye on her so that she doesn't jump off," she tells the old man before picking up the reins.

The cart carries on down the road, rattling and juddering. There is a clucking hen by Liza's feet, with its legs tied up. Behind her are large metal milk pails.

They've caught her. Of course they've caught her. It's all over.

"It's no joke! You've covered ten kilometres and you're such a little thing!" The old man offers her a morsel of bread and cheese. "Eat this. You won't be home for a while. We'll do our rounds first."

Liza pushes his hand away in silence.

It starts to rain. The old man covers everything with tarpaulin to keep the rain off. It goes over the potatoes, Liza and the hen.

The cart draws to a halt for the fifth time. The milk pails clatter. The dairymaid tells the story of how she apprehended Liza for the fifth time. And for the fifth time lifts the tarpaulin to reveal her. Liza huddles in the corner. Curious eyes study her.

"What a pretty little thing! Did you say she was violent?"

"Like a wolf cub! She bit my finger."

"Very wild. She's Russian."

"Is she really? How interesting!"

Liza tries to hide behind the sack of potatoes. Wolf cub. They're staring at her as if she really were a wild beast in a cage. Good job they're not stuffing cigarette ends up her nostrils.

Maids crowd around the gate to the pension.

"I've caught her!" the dairymaid shouts triumphantly from some way off. "I've caught your *mademoiselle*. Here she is!"

Liza is taken down from the cart.

"They've called the police already. Everybody's been searching for her."

Liza shakes her head. Her knees grow weak. A maid catches her.

"Liza! Liza dear!" Natasha is crying loudly, hugging her and kissing her hair, face and hands. "My darling child, you've given me such a fright! I thought you'd drowned! Liza darling!"

Liza is carried through to the bedroom and put to bed.

"My God." Natasha is horrified. "Ten kilometres!"

"I should box your ears," says Uncle Sasha. "I'll have to keep you under lock and key from now on, just you wait."

Natasha kisses her again.

"Liza darling, why? Don't you like being with us?"

Liza manages to lift her eyelids.

"No," she says slowly. "I wanted to go to Le Havre. To get on a ship to Russia." She surprises herself with a sob. "To suffer."

"To suffer?" says Natasha.

"To suffer?" says Uncle Sasha. "So that's what it was all about. To suffer!" Uncle Sasha gently pinches her nose. "You silly billy. Do you think they would have made a fuss over you over there? They would've just shaved your head like a criminal's and then sent you to the Komsomol."

She can hear laughter in the room next door. Really? To Russia? To suffer?

Liza blushes and buries her face in her pillow. The shame of it! The absolute shame of it! Everyone knows. Everyone's laughing at her.

The wind rattles the shutters. The rain drums on the roof. Natasha tucks her in.

"Sleep, my darling. What a storm! What would you have done on your own, my little runaway? Don't cry now, don't cry. Sleep now, and may God keep you."

Liza lies alone in the dark. Streams of rainwater gurgle as they run down the roof. The wind rattles the shutters. Sea waves crash.

The shame of it! The absolute shame of it! They would have shaved my head… He pinched my nose…

Her pillow is wet with tears. They keep streaming and streaming, and there isn't anything she can do to stop them.

A ship is sailing from Le Havre, crossing the white stormy waves. While she's stuck here. And it's all over.

Liza is sleeping and tears stream down her face.

She is dreaming of a cold blue sunrise. Jagged red walls and colourful church domes glitter in the cold blue light. Gold crosses shimmer high in the sky.

This is Moscow. This is the Kremlin.

Liza stands alone in the middle of a big, empty square.

A troop of soldiers forms a semicircle around her. Their guns gleam. She hears the bolts click. The black muzzles point right at her.

An officer with a red star on his chest bellows out the order: "Fire!"

III

LIZA OPENED HER EYES and ran her hand across her forehead. She looked around in confusion, failing to recognize her room at first. Outside, night had fallen. The faint light of a street lamp shone dimly through the black branches. Rain drummed on the windowpanes.

"Russia," she said aloud. She listened to the sound of her voice as she spoke. "Russia." She shook her head. The recollections of her unhappy, dream-filled childhood had made her heart feel hot and heavy in her breast and her mouth go dry.

She switched on the light and looked at the clock.

"It's gone eight already… Why haven't they called me down to dinner?"

She opened her door. The feeling of anxiety hadn't quite gone away. Her knees felt weak and her head was spinning ever so slightly. She let her legs carry her. One false step and she'd end up splayed on the polished floor of the hallway.

She found it a little easier to walk on the rug covering the drawing-room floor. Liza paused to catch her breath.

"I'm like an old goose, unable to control my nerves! The shame of it…"

"She'll fall for it… She's stupid." She heard Nikolai's voice in the dining room.

"No, she's not stupid, not at all. She's just naïve."

"Same difference," Nikolai interrupted him. "She'll fall for it. Liza!" He shouted.

Liza pushed the door open and immediately, before even crossing the threshold, felt as if something had just taken place. Andrei was sitting at the table. His eyes were gleaming and his lips were pursed resolutely. Under the yellow glare of the light, his face looked much too pale.

"Who's stupid? Who's going to fall for what?" she wanted to ask, but she hadn't the time.

Nikolai rushed over to her and took her hands in his.

"Liza." He looked her straight in the eye. "Liza, you're my sister and I don't want to keep this from you. Liza…" He caught his breath. "I don't know how to tell you this… Listen, Andrei and I are members of a monarchist organization. And now I'm being sent to Russia!"

"To Russia?" she asked him, the blood draining from her lips.

"That's right, to Russia. To deliver some documents. It's a very important and dangerous mission. I'll be leaving any day now. I may be executed out there. I wanted to ask you…" He paused again. "I wanted to ask you. Do you want to come with me?"

Liza stood still before her brother. But it was no longer the same Liza that had only just walked into the dining room. It was the little girl from Trouville, the heroic little girl ready to sacrifice herself. Joy and dread steadily drained the blood from her heart. Could this really be true? Could everything she hadn't even dared to dream finally be happening?

"To Russia?"

Nikolai shook her by the hands.

"What's wrong with you? Don't you understand what I'm saying? Do you want to go with me to Russia?"

Liza jerked her hands away from him and threw her arms around his neck.

"I can't believe it! Can it be true? Can it really be true? Oh, Kolya, I'm so happy, my heart could burst!"

"Hold on, hold on a minute. We need to talk about this properly. So, you agree to come with me. Now, tell me—will you help me?"

"Yes, yes, yes! I'll do anything! I'll do anything I can—and anything I can't!"

"All right, all right, slow down. Listen to me. We need money for the trip. Big money. The kind of money that our organization doesn't have. So I've been instructed to raise it myself. I thought you might be able to help with this."

"Me? But I don't—"

"Stop interrupting. I know you don't have a million in the bank. But you can still help. Cromwell is in love with you…"

Late that night, as she was drawing the curtains, Liza looked up at the sky.

"Today is Christmas Eve. It's a holiday." The dim thought crossed her mind. "That's right, it's a holiday. A real holy day. But what about Crom? Oh, never mind that. I'm not doing it for my own sake, I'm doing it for Russia. All for Russia." Liza let out a deep sigh. And she almost felt that with that sigh her heart flew out of her breast and out into the cold, dark night, past the moon and the clouds, higher and higher, all the way up to the star of Bethlehem and all the way up to God...

IV

THE FAINT SOUND of chiming bells carried through the open window.

Music? Where could it be coming from?

Liza had never heard such gentle, resonant, moving music.

She lay in her bed, smiling, afraid to move. "More, more! I don't want it to end."

And the music poured through the open window, floated over her bed and filled the entire room.

Liza gingerly opened her eyes.

Light was streaming in through the gap in the curtains. Liza had never seen light like this before. It was quite wonderful. It wasn't moonlight or sunlight. It merged with the music so the air shimmered iridescently with sound and light.

And then the music suddenly stopped.

Liza got up and opened the window. Warm, humid air caressed her face and her bare shoulders.

The morning was light and foggy.

The sky was a bright blue, with iridescent clouds strewn across it. Liza leant out and looked down. A white, transparent, iridescent fog blanketed the entire garden, revealing the occasional jasmine bush or dark fir tree only momentarily, before enveloping it again. On a circular patch of emerald-green lawn, right in front of the house, sat an angel.

The angel was sitting on his haunches with his large white wings folded on his back, like a bird. The wind ruffled his long golden hair. His bright blue eyes were gazing at the bright blue sky with a pensive and confused look. Beside him, on the green grass, lay a golden lyre.

"An angel!"

Liza let out an involuntary gasp and ran downstairs just as she was, barefoot and wearing only her light nightdress.

"An angel! No, it can't be. They don't exist. It's a dream." Thought after thought ran through her head. Yet she could distinctly feel the coolness of the stone staircase, the gravel on the garden path pricking her feet painfully and the grass wet with dew.

She ran over to the angel in silence, afraid of startling him. But the angel didn't seem to notice her. He went on looking up at the sky pensively and quite indifferently. She got on her knees and embraced him. He was warm and soft and rustled gently.

"My dear angel!" she whispered, barely breathing through her tears of bliss. "My dear angel!"

The angel didn't even flinch. Indifferently, his blue eyes gazed at the blue sky. She pressed her cheek to his warm, white, rustling wings. She felt as if her heart were bursting, as if she were dying of joy.

"My dear angel!"

Liza woke up and opened her eyes.

What a beautiful, prophetic dream.

An angel had visited her in her dream. The angel had said to her, "Go." As though he were speaking to Joan of Arc. She looked out of the window.

"The sun is out today. Soon I'll see it from Moscow… The sun is better there, it's a Russian sun."

For a moment, she saw stars in her eyes—yellow, red and pink dots danced before her. Through the dots she glimpsed Andrei's face. Liza closed her eyes.

"No, I mustn't think of him. I mustn't think about him, I mustn't think about love." She shook her head. She was happy now. This was true happiness. She was perfectly happy and she didn't need anything else. Not Andrei, not love.

She heard a knock at the door and then in walked Dasha, wearing an overcoat and a hat with flowers.

"Farewell, *mademoiselle*. I'm leaving now. I've got my wages."

Liza recollected that Nikolai had wanted to get rid of the maid so that she wouldn't see them leave.

"Goodbye, Dasha. All the best."

But Dasha didn't move.

"It's not hard to find a position such as this. My wages were always late and I never got a moment's peace. As for *madame*, the less said, the better. But I'll miss you, *mademoiselle*. I feel ever so sorry for you… Well, I hope you grow up big and clever."

She bowed.

"Thank you, Dasha."

But Dasha lingered in the doorway.

"However can you bear to stay with those two, all by yourself? They're always whispering about something. Hiding in corners and whispering."

Could Dasha have overheard something of their plans?

"They're putting on a play for Shrove Tuesday," Liza rushed to explain.

Dasha snorted.

"A play? I can't see any good coming of their play." She paused. "I feel ever so sorry for you, *mademoiselle*. Truly, I love you and I'm sorry to be leaving you."

"I'm sorry too, Dasha." Liza reached over and rummaged about in the dresser. She pulled out a colourful silk scarf and held it out to Dasha. "Thank you, Dasha. Take this as a keepsake." She pressed Dasha's coarse hand in hers. "Goodbye, Dasha."

Dasha bowed again.

"Goodbye, *mademoiselle*. May the Lord keep you."

Liza closed the door behind her. All of a sudden she felt genuinely quite sad. Dasha had lived under the same roof as Liza and had loved her, but Liza hadn't an inkling. She could have gone and sat with her in the kitchen, which would have made things a little better. They had lived under one roof and seen each other every day, and yet Liza had no idea. That's what life was like. Nobody knew anything. She shook her head. It would have been better before, but now she didn't need any love. She didn't need any pity. Now she was truly happy.

Time had almost stopped. The clocks were impossibly slow. Liza counted down the hours, the minutes until Saturday. Saturday night was when they were due to depart. Time had almost stopped, and the hour hand barely moved. This slow, halted existence was nothing but excited, happy anticipation. Liza had felt her heart ignited by Kolya's words on Christmas Eve: "Do you want to go to Russia?"—and still it went on smouldering in her breast. Her only fear was that it would flare up and burn her from the inside out.

V

CROMWELL WAS SITTING on the divan in Liza's room.

"You'll have the diamonds tomorrow night," he said.

Liza closed her eyes and leant her head back against the cushion. After a whole day of worrying and fussing, everything now felt still and quiet. She only had to wish for something in order to get it.

Like in a dream.

Cromwell was silent. Liza sat quietly, with her hands on her lap. Her heart was beating lightly and happily. Everything was fine, everything was splendid. And what lay ahead?

Cromwell cleared his throat.

"Are you unwell, Crom? Do you have a cold? That would be awful."

"No, I'm quite well." He looked her straight in the eyes. "You'll have the diamonds and the money tomorrow night," he repeated.

"Crom, you're an angel."

He shook his head sadly.

"Angels don't steal."

"Is it so hard for you to steal?"

"Terribly," he said earnestly. "It would be easier to die."

"How can stealing be more difficult than dying?"

Cromwell hung his head.

"It's far more difficult."

Liza looked at him with curiosity.

"I can't understand that. I'm afraid of dying."

She closed her eyes again and laid her head down on the cushion.

Before her she saw Andrei's pale, sad, angry face floating, as though in a haze.

"I would die only for love," she said quietly.

She felt a lump in her throat, and her hands grew cold.

"Or if I were executed. Or if I got sick, had an accident or died of old age."

Cromwell said nothing.

Her head rested on the cushion. Her face had acquired an expression of calm, distance, serenity. Quite inanimate, the life had drained out of it. Her lips were still and her eyelids tightly closed.

Cromwell leant over her. His heart contracted with pity. What was wrong with her? She was a girl, practically a child.

Why did she look so unhappy?

"Has some tragedy befallen you, Isolde?"

She opened her eyes. Her eyes shone brightly. Just for a moment, Cromwell felt as he had done back in Biarritz—her gaze caressed his skin like warm sunlight. And, just as he had done in Biarritz, he closed his eyes.

"Tragedy?" Liza asked, her voice ringing out brightly. "No, not tragedy—happiness, great happiness. We're going to Russia! I've never felt so happy."

They sat in silence for a while. Liza reached out and took his hand. He pressed her fingers in his.

"I'll bring everything tomorrow. But you won't forget, will you, Isolde? You won't forget what you promised me?"

She blushed.

"I'll remember. But we don't need to talk about that now. You see, Crom, Russia is blanketed in snow right now. Bright white snow. In the mornings the sunlight makes it look pink, and at night the moon turns it almost blue. You've never seen snow like it before. It exists only in Russia. Aren't you glad to be going?"

"Of course. Of course, I'm glad, Isolde."

The door opened and in walked Nikolai.

"Hullo, Crom." He squeezed Cromwell's shoulder affectionately. "Has it been arranged? When is it happening?"

"Tomorrow night."

"Excellent. We knew we could depend on you." He paused to think. "So, we can be on our way the day after tomorrow. You can spend the day here with us. There's no point in your going back home afterwards, in case they discover something."

Cromwell nodded.

"No, I shan't be able to go home after that."

Nikolai lit a cigarette.

"So, it's settled. Andrei!" he called out. "Andrei, come up here!"

They heard the rapid patter of footsteps coming up the stairs.

"We're leaving on Saturday!" shouted Liza.

Andrei had just entered; he was standing in the doorway.

"On Saturday?" he said in a strangled voice. His face was white as a sheet.

Liza walked over to him.

"What's the matter, Andrei? Are you unwell?"

He placed his hand on his heart.

"No, no, I just ran up too quickly, that's all. So, Saturday?" he asked again quietly. His voice sounded strangled and his lips were quavering.

Liza suddenly felt that she too was finding it difficult to breathe, as if she had also run up the stairs too quickly.

"He loves me," she thought. "He's jealous. He can't stand the thought of Crom going with me."

Nikolai held up his arm.

"Listen, chaps—how about we all go out to dinner one last time? Do you have any money, Crom?"

Cromwell nodded.

"I do."

"Wonderful. Let's have one last hurrah. Go and get ready, Liza."

"What nonsense," Andrei suddenly declared. "We're not going anywhere. We can't."

"Why not?" Liza asked in surprise.

"Because we can't be seen together." Andrei shrugged. "It may not matter to you, seeing as you're all leaving. But I'm the one who has to stay."

"He's right," Nikolai concurred. "We can't go out to a restaurant, but we needn't be dull either. Let's buy some wine and have a party here. Agreed?"

"Agreed."

VI

THE FIRE IS LIT in the dining room. A yellow light hangs low over the table.

Liza is sitting on the divan, her feet tucked under her. Her head is filled with noise. The hot, smoky air stings her eyes. Through the haze, she can see shiny glass bottles standing beside a plate of pink ham. Orange peel litters the floor. Nikolai pours her some more wine. She raises her glass.

"To our success! Why don't you want to clink glasses with me, Andrei?"

Andrei puts his glass down on the table.

"You can clink glasses with Cromwell. I've had too much to drink."

Liza shrugs.

"Suit yourself. Crom, to our success!"

Andrei laughs.

Liza drinks the wine and the noise in her head grows even louder.

The branches swaying outside the window look like hands reaching out towards her, pleading for help.

Car horns in the street sound like voices calling out to her: "We're waiting! We're waiting! Come on!"

"I'm coming!" she wants to shout back.

She reaches out her hand and plucks an apple from the fruit bowl.

She no longer has a heart in her breast. It's empty and silent there. Her heart is this red apple. This is it—her heart. It's sitting in the palm of her hand. It's exposed, it's beating, it flutters and it loves. It feels everything. She squeezes it with her fingers, and her heart feels pain. What should she do with it? What should she do with her heart?

She holds the apple out to Andrei.

"Eat this, Andrei, it's a gift from me to you."

Andrei takes the apple indifferently, rubs it on his sleeve and then digs his strong white teeth into it, taking a big bite.

"This pain is going to be horrible," Liza thinks. "He's eating my heart." She clenches her fists to stifle a cry of pain. But it doesn't hurt at all. She looks at Andrei in surprise and watches his white teeth chomp on the apple. And it doesn't hurt at all. "It's not my heart. I'm just drunk. Drop it. Don't eat it, Andrei."

Andrei throws the apple core on the floor.

Nikolai is laughing and drinking. And Cromwell, too, is laughing and drinking. Only Andrei is pale and sullen.

Liza quietly sings an old French song:

Écoutez ma chanson, dames et demoiselles.
Si vous mangez mon cœur, il vous poussera des ailes.[*]

Only Andrei hadn't eaten her heart; he'd eaten an apple.
If he'd eaten her heart, he'd be happy. The car horns
outside are calling her again: "We're waiting! We're
waiting! Come on!" Where do they want to take her? To
Russia? But she's going there already. In two days' time,
in two days' time. She presses her hands to her breast.
She's going to be a martyr. That's right, a martyr. She's
a heroine. She's going to save Russia. She's Joan of Arc.
An angel had come to her in a dream and said: "Go."
She clenches her fists tighter and gets up from the divan.
The ringing in her ears grows louder. It's the ringing of
church bells in Moscow. She feels so light, so ethereal,
so happy. If she were to wave her arms, she would fly up
to the sky. But she can't fly up to the sky. She is needed
here, on earth. She has to save Russia, for that is why she
was put on this earth.

She goes right up to the fireplace. Why is it so hot? Is
it the fire there or the one burning in her breast?

"I'm going to Petersburg, as well," she hears Nikolai say.

Petersburg… She turns around and looks at Andrei,
Nikolai and Cromwell. They're sitting on the divan,

* *Écoutez… ailes*: "Hear my song, ladies and damsels. If you eat my heart,
it will give you wings."

drinking. Cromwell strikes a match. The yellow flame flickers feebly amid the smoky air.

Petersburg…

She watches Andrei suddenly start to dissolve, to melt away, to stretch taller and taller.

It's not Andrei any more. It's a tall mast with a big white flag fluttering on top of it. The room, the cigarette smoke and the bottles are all gone.

There is a blue river, a blue sky, hundreds of white flags billowing on top of masts. There are so many ships, so many flags, so many seagulls. No, it's not Petersburg. It's Constantinople. It's Marseilles. Liza shakes her head.

"No, it's not Petersburg."

Nikolai is standing in the middle of the room.

"Then I'll have to go to Kiev for a few days before going back to Moscow…"

He's waving his arms and Andrei is laughing.

"What a fabulous, what a dangerous journey you're undertaking! You're a hero!"

Nikolai spins round and scowls at him.

"Are you drunk?"

"Not at all. In fact, I'm going to have another drink." Andrei pours himself some more wine. "Drink with me." He holds up his glass and clinks it with Cromwell's. "To your journey!" He looks him straight in the eyes. "To your journey to hell!"

"To hell?" Cromwell is taken aback.

"Are you drunk?" Nikolai grabs Andrei's glass out of his hand. "Don't you dare drink a drop more!"

"You're the one who's drunk, not me." Andrei makes himself more comfortable on the divan. He brings his pale, angry face close to Cromwell's. "Naturally, you're going to hell. Isn't today's Russia hell?"

Liza watches him. He's so handsome! She sits down beside him and places her hand on his shoulder.

"You know, Andrei…"

But he isn't listening to her. He's looking Cromwell up and down, looking at his long legs stretching out from the divan.

"I'm afraid the suitcases will be too small," he says in Russian.

Nikolai shakes him by the shoulder. He's bright red and his lips are trembling.

"You're drunk. Shut up this minute! You're mad."

"And you're a coward. You thought it all up and now you're frightened."

Liza's eyes open wide in incomprehension.

"What are you talking about? What suitcases?"

"Don't worry about it, Liza. Don't take any notice of him," Nikolai reassures her. "Andrei's drunk. We ought to go to bed."

"To bed?" Liza stretches her arms. "Already? And we were having such a lovely time."

"Liza," Nikolai says sternly. "You haven't forgotten, have you?"

Liza shakes her head.

"No, no, I haven't forgotten anything."

Indeed, she hadn't forgotten anything. The day after tomorrow they were going to Russia.

She staggers to her feet. Her legs have grown so heavy!

"Go home, Crom dearest. It's late. You have a difficult day ahead of you."

Cromwell is practically asleep already. His head is resting on the cushion. His eyes are shut.

"Crom, it's time to go home."

"Yes, yes, I'm going. It's been such fun. When we return from Russia, we can see each other often—"

"We can talk about that later. Go home now."

Nikolai shakes his hand.

"Goodnight and goodbye."

"Till tomorrow."

They all walk him to the hallway. The glare from the light high up near the ceiling is intolerable. Everything is swaying and spinning. Nikolai helps Cromwell into his coat.

"Will you be all right on your own? Should I see you home?"

Cromwell smiles gratefully.

"Thank you, you're so kind. You're all so very kind."

Andrei suddenly laughs again very loudly, startling Liza.

"What's the matter with you?"

"Goodnight." Cromwell bows to them. "I'll walk myself home just fine. Goodnight, Isolde."

The door slams shut behind him.

"You're an idiot!" Nikolai shouts angrily.

"And you're a coward!"

"Stop arguing and go to bed."

Liza goes to the staircase and places her foot on the first step. Her ears are ringing, her vision grows dim. She can't make sense of anything. And she doesn't need to. She just needs to make it to her room, she just needs to lie down and fall asleep.

VII

ORDINARILY LIZA would wash upstairs in her room, but after last night she felt like she needed a bath. Her head ached and she had a horrible metallic taste in her mouth. Liza frowned. It was a bad business, she really must stop drinking like this.

White suds fell on the floor. A cloud of steam rose from the hot water. The yellow electric light shone dimly on the wall, like a street lamp in fog.

Liza didn't like the bathroom. It was narrow and dark and had no windows, only a small door upholstered in felt. Liza always thought that it was more like a prison cell or a crypt than a bathroom. She also thought it smelt of damp, bogs and dead toads, although there were no bogs or toads to be had there. The bathroom would have been well suited for chaining up one's enemies. They could scream all they liked and nobody would hear them.

Liza put on her house robe and slippers and went out into the hallway. She should make some tea now that Dasha was gone. She could hear voices in the dining room. Kolya was already up and Andrei was with him.

She wanted to join them. "No, I'll go and make some tea first. They must be hungry."

She ran along the corridor to the kitchen. Dirty pots crowded the stove, crumpled napkins littered the floor.

"What a mess, and Dasha's only been gone a day!" She opened the back door and picked up a loaf of bread that had been delivered from the baker's that morning.

"I'm being helpful and useful. Kolya will be impressed!"

The water came to a noisy boil. Liza picked up the kettle from the stove, tucked the bread under one arm and took the sugar bowl in her free hand. Slowly and carefully, she made her way down the corridor. Her felt slippers carried her noiselessly. Liza was proud of herself. It was only tea, a trifling thing, but she was being helpful.

The bread almost slipped out from under her arm and she stopped to catch it. She pressed it to her breast and suddenly heard Nikolai's voice from behind the door:

"You have to shoot from behind, in the back. And the muzzle has to be covered."

Liza pushed the door open.

Andrei was standing by the window, holding a revolver in his hand.

Nikolai was leaning over it and wrapping his handkerchief around the muzzle. They both spun around to look at her when the door creaked open. Their eyes had the same black haunted expression.

Liza dropped the bread on the floor and her hands started shaking, making the tin lid of the kettle jump.

"Who are you going to shoot in the back?"

Nikolai was furious.

"What are you doing eavesdropping at the door?"

"I wasn't eavesdropping. I've made you tea."

But Nikolai was already calm. He hid the revolver in his pocket.

"All right, all right. Put the kettle on the table. We don't want you scalding yourself. Come and have some tea, Andrei."

Andrei picked the bread up off the floor.

"It's a sin to drop bread on the floor. That's what Nanny taught me. Why are you staring at me like that, Liza?"

"Who are you shooting in the back?" Liza repeated.

"Oh, you're still harping on about that!" Nikolai laughed. "Whoever I need to. A border guard or a Cheka man. You don't think I'm going to Russia to catch butterflies or have a snowball fight, do you?"

Liza shook her head.

"But why do you need to wrap the muzzle with a handkerchief?"

Nikolai stirred sugar into his tea.

"So you can't hear the gunshot. The shot always has to be silent."

Liza sat down at the table in silence. The tablecloth was stained with patches of dark red wine. Her hands started shaking again. Kolya was right, of course—what did she have to be so frightened of?

"We need you to go to the station right away, Liza, to find out the train times. Can you do that?"

Liza nodded. She tried not to look at Andrei, Nikolai or the dark stains on the tablecloth. She got up.

"Fine, I'll go now."

Liza dressed in a hurry. In the hallway, she strained her ears to see whether she could make out anything else being said in the dining room, but they had begun to whisper.

VIII

WHEN LIZA returned home, she found Nikolai sitting by the window.

"It's at ten-thirty!" Liza shouted. "The train's at ten-thirty!"

"The train?" Nikolai asked, confused.

"Yes, the train. The train to Moscow!" Liza laughed. "What's wrong with you, are you asleep?"

"No, I'm thinking."

"There's one in the morning, too."

"We don't need the morning one. Thanks for finding out anyway. Ten-thirty, you said?"

"Yes. Where's Andrei?"

"He's gone home."

"Why? He always stays with us these days."

"Well, he couldn't tonight."

Liza shrugged.

"But it's our last night… We're leaving tomorrow."

"His aunt has visitors. Stop asking questions."

Liza said nothing.

The table was still laden with empty bottles, dirty plates and used glasses. Liza began to feel a bit nauseated again. It had been such fun asking about trains to Moscow at the station, as if she were about to leave, and proceeding to run around various shops, looking at gloves and stockings that she might buy to wear there. But here at home she felt wretched; it was probably the mess. She set to work.

"Hold on, Kolya, let me tidy up a bit. It's like a pigsty in here."

"Don't bother, it isn't worth it."

"Crom will be here soon."

"Well, we needn't worry about him any more."

"Why not?" She was surprised.

She hastily cleared the table.

"Oh, do stop your fussing! Listen, Liza…" Nikolai paused for a moment. "Don't forget—Cromwell is sleeping in your room tonight."

Liza blushed.

"I promised him, but…"

"No," Nikolai interrupted her. "He must. You'll take him straight up to your room."

A glass fell out of Liza's shaking hand and smashed on the floor with a final, pitiful ring.

"I've broken it!" Liza cried out in fright. "But it's all right. It was a clear glass, so it's a good omen."

Nikolai grabbed her by the shoulder.

"Crom has to sleep in your room, do you understand?"

Liza nodded obediently.

"Fine, but why? We could just put him up in the drawing room."

Nikolai frowned in irritation.

"Please, no more questions. Just do as I say."

Liza nodded again.

"Fine."

The evening dragged on and on, with no end in sight. Nikolai smoked in silence. Liza sat on the divan, with her feet tucked under her.

"I do wish you'd make a fire, Kolya, it's so cold!"

"Oh, leave me in peace!" He threw his cigarette down on the floor, angrily. "I've got other things to worry about. What time did Cromwell say he'd be here?"

"He said as soon as his mother fell asleep. At about eleven."

"Eleven! That's a long wait, still."

They fell silent again. Liza looked at the yellow light, then at the thick, dull coating of dust on the sideboard.

"Kolya, I'm hungry. I haven't eaten anything all day."

Nikolai shrugged.

"You're a big girl, you can look after yourself. There's ham and bread in the kitchen."

Liza went through to the kitchen, switched on the gas and put the kettle on the stove.

"What's weighing so heavily on me?" she wondered.

"What am I afraid of? Everything is just fine, everything is splendid. We're leaving tomorrow. So what is it then?"

But her heart felt large and heavy, as if it were not a heart, but a stone weight in her breast. Her knees grew weak and her hands shook.

Liza cut some bread, topped it with a slice of ham and started eating it just as she stood there next to the stove. But she found it difficult to swallow. Her throat had closed up too much. She didn't want to eat any more.

She put the bread back on the plate and shook her head. "Why do I feel like this? Only a minute ago I was hungry."

She made her way back along the long corridor and sat down on the divan. Nikolai was still smoking—angrily, silently. Everything was quiet. Outside, the moon shone through the black naked branches. Liza clasped her cold hands together and quite unexpectedly heard herself say:

"Kolya, I'm frightened. I'm scared."

Her voice was loud and anxious.

Nikolai turned to look at her.

"You're scared?" he asked sharply. "It's too early to be scared."

"What? Too early? What are you saying?"

"Nothing. Shut up. There's nothing for you to be scared of."

"Kolya…" Liza whispered. "I can't. I'm so scared today, it's like every corner has a—"

"Shut up!" Nikolai turned pale and his lips trembled. He quickly looked over his shoulder. "Shut up. I may be scared too, for all you know."

"Kolya…" Liza pressed her cold hands to her breast and closed her eyes. It grew very quiet. All she could hear was the blood pounding in her ears.

Nikolai moved his chair aside forcefully. She heard the flick of the light switch, and a bright light appeared right above her head. Liza opened her eyes.

"Nonsense. There's nothing to be frightened of." Nikolai was still pale. He wanted to smile, but his lips couldn't manage it. "You're such a scaredy-cat, Liza. You wouldn't say boo to a goose!"

He closed the shutters and drew the yellow curtains.

"It's just the dark, the silence, the waiting around… Don't be scared. There's nothing to be afraid of. Let's turn the lights on in the drawing room, as well."

He brought her a shawl.

"Wrap yourself in this. You're cold. You'll be much more relaxed when you warm yourself up."

He set the gramophone going.

"Music! Just the thing. Now we have light, warmth and music. You're not still scared, are you, Liza?"

Liza sat in the corner of the divan. The thick shawl lay across her motionless legs. Her eyes squinted in the bright electric light. The shrill strains of a foxtrot assaulted her ears.

"This is every bit as good as a dance hall," said Nikolai, smiling quite calmly now. "And just to make it even more fun, why don't we have a dance, my little sparrow?"

He proffered his hand.

She was about to get up—there was nothing to be scared of, after all—when suddenly she saw the shadow his hands cast on the wall. The shadow was enormous, dark and grotesque. His arms were reaching out to get her; the long, bony fingers on his hands were trying to get at her throat. She pressed herself back into the divan.

"Don't touch me! Don't touch me! Leave me alone!"

Nikolai recoiled in shock.

"What? What's the matter with you? Why are you screaming as if I'm trying to slit your throat?"

But Liza went on screaming, terrified of the shadows, which were still stretching their fingers out towards her.

"Don't touch me! I'm scared! I'm scared of you!"

IX

THAT EVENING was spent just like every other evening when they both stayed in. They read in silence, gently interrupting each other every now and again just to exchange a few words. Their drawing room was quiet and cosy, with a large roaring fire and low, comfortable armchairs. It was more like a room in a wealthy English home than a large Parisian hotel.

At half past ten, Cromwell's mother set her book to one side and got up from her armchair.

"Goodnight, Cromwell. You should go to bed, it's late."

Cromwell got up too. The opalescent light cast a soft glow over his worried face. His mother studied him closely.

"Is something the matter, Cromwell? You seem rather out of sorts. Are you quite well?"

Cromwell blushed.

"I have a headache," he said quietly.

She pressed her hand against his forehead.

"You don't have a fever. Go and get some sleep. You'll feel better again in the morning."

He silently kissed her hand. She pressed her lips to his smooth cheek.

"You'll have to start shaving soon," she smiled. "My son is quite grown-up now," she thought to herself.

"Go to bed and leave your books until tomorrow," she said.

She walked over to her bedroom and paused in the doorway, while Cromwell switched the lights off in the drawing room. Then she gave him a little nod and went through.

"My son. He's grown so tall and so handsome!"

The white sheets and lilac covers were folded back over her vast bed.

Slowly, she undressed. Her dress was draped over the armchair. A long pearl necklace gently collapsed into the padded velvet drawer of her jewellery box. She took off her rings and earrings, brushed back her short hair and studied her reflection in the dresser mirror. Her face was beautiful. Cold, but still young. Her neck was slender, and her shoulders pale.

"I'm a lucky woman," she thought to herself. "I'm so, so happy. I have someone to live for. Cromwell—my boy."

She lay down, pulled the covers over herself and stretched out her long, muscular legs.

"Tomorrow morning I'm going riding in the Bois de Boulogne," she remembered with pleasure. "And then lunch at Jen's. How lovely."

She lay on her back and crossed her arms over the covers to say her bedtime prayers.

After she'd finished, she turned over to lie on her right side and closed her eyes.

Sleep drew so near. Her head was filled with snatches of words and phrases. They were floating around like scraps of clouds in an otherwise empty sky. She didn't have the strength to string them together, to make sense of what they meant. But suddenly, her shoulders shook in a violent shudder. Startled, she opened her eyes.

"Cromwell!" she said loudly. An anxiety, an animal instinct pulsated through her whole body until she felt unable to breathe. It was a mother's fear for her offspring. "Cromwell."

Her heart clenched, as it always did when her son was ill or in danger. The familiar sensation of fear echoed painfully throughout her body. That unforgettable, terrible pain that she felt when he was born—the first moments of his life, when the blood bond connecting mother and child had yet to be severed.

She sat up and passed her hand over her forehead.

"What's happening to me? Cromwell is home. He's sleeping. He's well. I've nothing to be worried about. It's just my nerves," she whispered, twisting her mouth into the same scornful smile as Cromwell's whenever he referred to "nerves".

She switched on the lamp that stood on her bedside table and took a sip of water.

"I must just be tired. Thankfully, we've only a week left before we go home. This trip has lasted long enough." Cromwell. She needn't worry about Cromwell. It's true that Leslie had seen him in questionable company in a restaurant one night, with horrid girls and horrid boys, but that kind of thing was understandable at his age. And when she raised it with him, he apologized. His teacher was very satisfied with his progress. He was a kind, honourable boy. He was just like his father. Everything was fine. She needn't worry.

She laid her head back on the pillow and closed her eyes.

"That being said, I'll be so glad to see Cromwell back at Eton," she thought as she drifted off to sleep.

Through sleep, she heard the door squeak gently and someone walk into the room. She woke up.

"A thief," she knew instantly. Still half-asleep and without opening her eyes, she reached for the revolver under her pillow and clasped the cold steel with her fingers. She was not afraid. She was brave and always felt elated in the face of danger, as when she and her husband had hunted lions, and that time in Switzerland when she had fallen from a cliff into a crevasse.

She lay stock-still, breathing steadily and listening to every noise. Then she moved her head as if she were still asleep and carefully opened her eyes.

The room was almost pitch-black. Only the opalescent light on her bedside table gave off a dim glow.

She saw Cromwell, his arms outstretched like a blind man's, moving on tiptoe towards her dressing table. She didn't move or cry out; she just unclenched her fingers from the revolver.

Cromwell stopped, opened her jewellery box and then opened the drawer of her bureau and started stuffing something quickly into his pockets.

She carried on breathing evenly and calmly. He turned to look at his mother, his eyes darting and squinting with anxiety.

"He squints," she thought quite calmly, as if he were a stranger. "I've never noticed before that he squints."

As if Cromwell's possible squint was the only thing that interested her at that moment in time.

The drawing-room light went out and the door to the corridor quietly closed.

That's when she got up and walked over to her dressing table. She still couldn't quite believe it. Perhaps he had come by just to borrow a book. But her jewellery box was empty and the money from the bureau was gone.

"Thief!" she cried out. "Cromwell is a thief." She listened to the sound of her own voice.

In the dark mirror, she caught a glimpse of her pale, instantly aged face and turned away in horror and disgust.

"I'm the mother of a thief. The mother of a thief."

She remembered how a few years ago she had gone to see a scandalous trial. A young man from a good family had robbed a bank. All of London was in court that day. The mother of the thief—an old lady in mourning—wouldn't stop crying. He was sentenced to ten years in prison. It had been hot and boring, and she regretted going. Back then, she thought that there were two kinds of people: honest folk and criminals. And that between them lay the deepest crevasse. And she found everything that concerned criminals to be uninteresting and distasteful. She never spared them a moment's thought. She didn't even pity the weeping old woman in mourning. Why would the mother of a thief deserve pity?

"And now Cromwell is a thief," she repeated. "A thief."

There was no crevasse any more, everything had mixed together and he was now on the other side, with the criminals. And she, his mother, was there too. He was her son. James's son.

"What a blessing that James was killed," she whispered and burst into tears.

What was she to do? What was she going to do now? She cried and cried until she was weak from weeping. There was nothing she could do.

"We'll leave for London tomorrow," she finally decided. "Tomorrow morning, I'll speak to him. I have to wait till morning to calm myself down. There's no going back now anyway." Even if nobody were to find out about this, even if he were not sentenced to hard labour, he was going to remain a thief for ever. And she would never forget that she was the mother of a thief.

She got back into bed. As she pulled up the cover, her hand brushed her naked breast and immediately recoiled in disgust, as if she had touched a toad, so repulsive was her naked body to her.

X

LIZA OPENED the door to Cromwell. He entered the house quickly—as if he were on the run—and double-locked the door behind him. They stood facing one another, pale and confused.

"Did you get them?" Liza said, her voice breaking with anxiety.

"Here." He held out a long string of pearls, as he began taking out wads of notes from his pockets.

"Wait, Crom, where am I supposed to put all this? Let's go up to my room and you can give me it all there. Take off your coat."

He stuffed the crumpled notes back into his pockets obediently.

Liza walked on ahead. The string of pearls hung off her wrist like a rosary.

"Quiet! Kolya is asleep already."

"Asleep?" he asked in disbelief when they reached the landing.

"Yes, sleeping. What's so odd about that?" She glanced at him over her shoulder. He was clambering laboriously up the stairs. The look on his face was quite different from usual—it was tired and resigned. Liza switched the light on.

"Take a seat on the divan, Crom. Was it difficult?"

"Yes, very. But I thought it would have been even worse."

"She didn't wake up?"

"No, she was asleep. She didn't even stir." He paused for a moment. "But she'll know tomorrow…" he added, his voice trailing off.

Liza sat down beside him. She wanted to comfort him, to reassure him. But he didn't need comforting. No, what she needed to do, what she absolutely must do, was say something to him. But what? What?

He stood up, pulled the money, earrings and rings out of his pockets and piled them on her desk.

Liza didn't even turn to look at them.

"Listen, Crom." She clasped her arms around her knees. "Crom, you know, I don't think you should go to Russia after all."

"Why ever not?"

"I don't know. But you shouldn't. I'm scared for you, Crom," she whispered. "I'm scared for you," she repeated, and those words suddenly clarified everything for her—the anxiety that had gripped her all day, that inexplicable fear. It was all clear to her now—she was scared for Cromwell's sake. She didn't yet understand what danger lay in store for him, but she knew that it was imminent.

She got up and walked over to him.

"Crom, you must leave. It's still not too late. Crom! Your mother's still asleep."

She quickly gathered up the money and jewellery from the desk.

"Take it. Take it back. Take it home. Go home, Crom. Nobody has to know anything. Go home."

He looked at her in astonishment.

"What are you talking about? I thought you said…?"

She took his hand in hers.

"Crom, please. Go home, Crom. I know it was me who talked you into this. But I didn't understand anything then. You don't need this. You should stay out of it. You're an Englishman, Crom. Take the pearls, take the money and go home."

He shook his head.

"Stop it, Liza."

"Crom, I'm begging you—go home."

She tried to stuff the money back into his pockets. He took her hands in his and bent down to look into her eyes.

"This isn't how brave young women behave."

"If you love me, Crom, please… I'm begging you."

"No, I won't. I won't, precisely because I love you. It's too late now anyway. It's too late for me. I'm a thief. The only thing I have left in my life is you."

"Oh, Crom, but you haven't thought it through! They could kill you in Russia."

"But they could kill you, too! We'll be together. I'm so unhappy here. I don't much value life at all."

He put his arms around her.

"Kiss me, Liza. Don't let's talk about it any more."

She lifted her face to his and gazed into his pale-blue eyes. They were just like a baby's. Overwhelmed by tenderness, fear and pity, she felt his hot lips on hers. And suddenly, through the kiss, through the blood pounding in her ears, through all the tenderness and pity, she heard a faint noise. A barely audible noise. Liza threw her head back and, still fixing the gaze of the pale-blue baby's eyes, trained her ears. She heard something click on the other side of the door. And then all was still.

What was that? She pressed her lips to his again and threw her arms around his neck; growing weak from fear, pity and tenderness, she held on to him to prevent herself from falling.

"You've gone terribly pale. Do you feel unwell?"

"No, not at all. Kiss me again, Crom darling."

She pressed herself to him but then quickly removed her arms from his neck and withdrew.

"Wait here. Sit down on the divan."

"You're leaving?"

"No, no, just wait a minute, Crom. I'll be right back."

She walked over to the door quietly and gently pressed the door handle. The door didn't move.

"It's locked," she thought. "It's locked from the outside, on the latch."

Without saying a word, she went over, opened the curtains and threw open the windows. Bright moonlight illuminated the garden and the smooth stretch of wall beneath her window. There was no ledge, no drainpipe. Jumping would mean breaking one's legs.

She closed the window and drew the curtains together.

"Crom could break the door down. He's stronger than Nikolai. And I'd help him," she thought.

Cromwell reached his hand out towards her.

"Come here, Isolde. What are you looking at over there?"

"Crom, I'm asking you for the last time. Go home."

He shook his head.

"Enough. I'm not going anywhere. Even if I had to die in an hour, I wouldn't leave you."

Liza let out a sigh.

"All right. If you don't want to, then…" She paused. "Then let's go to bed, Crom. It's very late," she added quickly, blushing.

She was embarrassed.

"We'll go to bed with our clothes on, all right? The divan's very big."

He blushed too. He looked at her uncertainly.

She fetched a pillow and a blanket from the cupboard.

"Will you be able to sleep in your clothes?"

"Of course I shall."

"There's only one pillow, so we'll have to put our heads close together. Will you be comfortable enough? What is it? Go to bed now."

He lay down against the wall. She lay down beside him and turned out the light.

"Are you all right, Crom? Are you warm enough?"

"Yes, thank you."

"You're so long. Your arms are so strong. If you're uncomfortable, you can get undressed."

She pressed herself against him in the dark.

"No, I'm comfortable like this."

"Crom. My darling Crom," she whispered into his ear. "I love you so, so much. I'm so grateful to you. If you wanted something, I wouldn't say no, Crom."

He moved away from her, even pushing her away her a little.

"No, not that, that's not allowed." There was fear in his voice.

"But why? Why not? What if I want it? I want you to be happy."

He embraced her again.

"I am happy." He kissed her cold cheek. "When we get back from Russia, when we're grown-up, then we can marry."

"Oh, Crom, we'll never grow up."

"Who knows? We could live to a hundred."

"No, no. Anyway, why wait? Why always wait? Why don't you want it now? Why?"

"Because it's not allowed."

He leant over her in the dark and kissed her neck, her lips, her eyes.

"You're crying. Why are you crying, Isolde?"

"Because we have so little time left to live."

He fell asleep before she did. His head rested heavily on her shoulder. She remained absolutely still, so as not to wake him. Tears were still trickling down her face. She had never felt such pity, such tenderness, such weakness. Grey light streamed in through the slightly parted curtains.

She gazed at his sleeping face. She was thinking of nothing in particular, nothing crossed her mind. He was asleep. He was breathing steadily, and was so warm. Just like a child. She tucked the blanket more snugly under his chin.

"He's just like a baby. Like he's my son. Sleep, sleep, little darling." And she closed her eyes, still smiling.

When Liza woke up, Cromwell was already gone, and the money and diamonds were no longer on the desk.

She made her way downstairs. Cromwell, Andrei and Nikolai were taking breakfast in the dining room. Eggs and bacon were frying in a pan on the stove. Nikolai was pouring the coffee. He seemed very pleased. Liza bid them good morning and sat down at her place.

Nikolai was looking after Cromwell.

"Why aren't you eating? Shall I fry you a steak?"

"Thank you, I'm full."

But Nikolai insisted.

"You must eat. You're used to hearty breakfasts. It'll set you up for the journey…"

For the journey. Liza imagined a train with Russian yellow, blue and green carriages. This was the train that was going to take her to Russia.

"Liza, why aren't you eating? Do you need an invitation?"

Liza looked at her brother with surprise. He was being so nice. She hadn't seen him like this for a long time.

"It's because we're finally leaving. And that's why Andrei is sulking, too," she thought as she gulped down her hot coffee. "As for Kolya locking my door, he was right to do so. I very nearly ruined everything."

She lifted her head.

"If we're leaving tonight, then when am I going to buy stockings and sweaters?"

Nikolai laughed.

"Oh, you're on about sweaters again. I suppose everyone has priorities, and yours are sweaters. Go on, then, go and buy yourself some."

He took out two hundred-franc notes from his pocket.

"Make sure they're warm."

"What about you?"

"We don't need any. We have some that we'll pick up at the border. Just make sure you're home by six."

Liza took the money.

"All right."

Nikolai got up.

"Listen, Crom, you should write to your mother."

Cromwell shrugged.

"Why?"

"So that she doesn't worry. Tell her you'll be back in three months. And that you didn't take the money and things for yourself, but for a…" Nikolai paused as he searched for the right words. "For a just cause."

"As if that would change anything! She won't care why I stole them."

"No, no," Nikolai was eager to convince him. "It changes everything. You must write. Tell him, Liza."

Liza nodded.

"Of course. Crom, you should write."

Cromwell thought for a moment.

"All right. If you insist. Give me some paper. I'll write, although it's hardly necessary now."

Liza watched his pen quickly cover the white page with unfamiliar black words.

He licked and sealed the envelope. Nikolai picked it up.

"Post it, Liza."

Liza went over to Cromwell.

"Do you want to come shopping with me, Crom?"

"He can't go out," Nikolai interrupted her. "He might be spotted, and then we'll be in trouble."

Liza sighed.

"Well, if you say so…" She took Cromwell's hand. "I really don't want to leave you today, Crom. Come, see me out."

In the hallway, he took her short coat with the gold buttons down from the stand and handed it to her.

She put on her beret and smiled at him.

"You were just like a baby last night. Like you were my son." She blushed. "Well, goodbye, Crom."

XI

IT WAS SIX O'CLOCK. Liza was making her way home, clutching a parcel to her chest.

Warm stockings. She could wear them to the North Pole if she wanted. And gloves too. She loved the sweater most of all though. Made of camel's wool, it was so fluffy and light! Although maybe she shouldn't have bought the pink one. Joan of Arc probably wouldn't have worn the pink one. But they didn't even have sweaters back in those days. And it was too late to change it anyway. "I'll have to tell Kolya that it was the only colour they had," she thought.

She took out her keys, unlocked the front door and stepped inside, into the dark hallway. A wall of damp air assaulted her nostrils.

It was as cold inside as it was out. The house didn't seem lived-in any more; it seemed abandoned. "Well, we're leaving tonight anyway."

"Hello!" she called out. Her voice was loud and carried. No reply came. The drawing room was empty. Cromwell was sitting in the dining room, under the hanging light, copying something out of a guidebook.

"Look what I bought!"

"Hold on, I'll take a look in a minute. Nikolai asked me to draw up our itinerary, but I don't understand some parts."

"Where are they?"

"Upstairs. They must be packing."

Liza ran upstairs.

"Kolya!" she called out.

Nikolai's bedroom door opened and Andrei stuck his head out.

"Leave us alone, we're busy."

"I wanted to show you my sweater."

"Later, you can do it later. You have one and that's all we need to know."

"Go downstairs," Nikolai shouted. "We'll need your help in a minute."

Liza went back to the dining room and sat down on the divan. She was still holding her parcel, which she placed on her lap. How cold it was! They could have made a fire… Never mind—she needed to get used to it. Russia was much colder.

Cromwell kept writing, rustling the pages of the guidebook.

Liza leant back against the wall. Everything was just like the night before. A thick layer of dust still coated the sideboard, dirty plates were still stacked on the stained tablecloth. And it was just as silent. And, probably because everything was just like the night before, she felt sad and anxious once again.

"We're leaving tonight."

But the thought offered her no comfort. Just as on the previous night, she felt anxiety seep into her blood with the cold. Her hands started shaking again.

"I know what this is. It's anxiety before a big journey. Everyone gets it. It even has a name—*Reisefieber*."

But her hands shook more and more, and her heart beat heavily and anxiously.

"Crom, are you finished?"

"Just a minute."

She heard the rustle of paper amid the silence. Liza sighed. How hard it was, how wearying.

She couldn't wait to get out of this abandoned house. The sooner the better. Andrei could at least come down to say goodbye. No, she must stop thinking about Andrei.

Why did she feel so anxious? What was weighing down on her so?

"Liza!" she heard Nikolai call out loudly.

Liza jumped to her feet and ran into the hallway. It was all going to be over now. They were going to start fussing and packing and then they'd leave. What was there to worry about? Everything was going to be all right.

Nikolai came down the stairs and walked over to her with long, decisive strides.

"Put your coat on," he said, his voice hoarse. "You're going to go out into the garden and if anybody comes, you're going to say that nobody is in and that you've locked yourself out and can't get in. Do you understand?"

"What?" Confused, she looked at him closely. Only then did she notice that he was very pale. "Why do I need to go out into the garden?"

"Stop asking questions, do you hear me? Don't you dare come back in until I've unlocked the door. Get your coat on now."

"I…" she whispered, as her legs started shaking, "I don't want to. I won't go. Why should I?"

He held her by the shoulder.

"You won't go?" he repeated slowly. But it wasn't Kolya any more, it wasn't her brother. It was a stranger, a frightening figure. A figure capable of anything. For the first time ever, Liza feared for her life.

He took her coat off the stand.

"Chop-chop. If anyone turns up, don't let them in. Understood?"

She took a long time putting her coat on. Her arms kept missing the sleeves. Fear constricted her throat, ran down her arms, her breast, her back, all the way down to her knees, making her legs feel hollow and weak, as if the bones had been taken out. She had no strength left to stand, her legs no longer held her up and she wanted to collapse onto the floor. But fear pounded her from the inside out: "Keep standing, keep standing. If you fall, it'll all be over."

She darted to the exit, but Nikolai barred her way.

"What about your hat and your gloves?"

She held out her trembling hand to receive her beret. He opened the door for her.

"Go on. And don't forget what I said."

As she passed him, she put all her concentration into staying upright.

"Don't let anyone in."

A light breeze struck her face. It was almost spring-like. She grabbed onto the handrail as she made her way down into the garden.

"What's going on? What am I doing here?"

She sat down on the bench and gripped its arms with both hands.

The trees inclined over her, swaying and slowly dissolving. The sky trembled and shook, and slowly lowered itself over the house, the garden and Liza herself, enveloping everything in a thick, cold grey fog. She felt as if she were at the bottom of a river, not in a garden, and surrounded by water, not fog.

Liza drew a deep breath and the fog flooded her open mouth, like water. She wanted to cry out, but the fog choked her. It enveloped her heart and her brain, and no longer did she feel frightened or distressed.

She rested her head against the back of the bench. It was just a dream.

"I must be dreaming."

The grey density of the fog was disturbed by a long black motor car. It moved through it slowly and silently, like a large fish. Large round headlights that looked like fish eyes shone out brightly.

"I must be dreaming," thought Liza in confusion. "This is all a dream—the fog, the garden, the motor car."

The motor car pulled up right beside the garden fence. A tall man in a grey overcoat climbed out. He pushed open the garden gate. Through the dream, through the fog, she saw Nikolai's angry face and heard his hoarse voice pronounce right in her ear: "Don't let anyone in."

She jumped up and her dream became reality. Or perhaps reality became her dream.

"Can I help you?" she called out.

"Is this where the Russians live?" asked the man in the grey coat.

"What Russians?"

He stepped towards her, straining to see her in the dark.

"Oh, it's you," he said in French. "You were in the restaurant that time, with Cromwell."

"You're that man. You're his cousin."

She recognized him too.

He nodded. The trees were swaying silently above his head. Two strips of light from the headlights cut across the darkness of the garden.

"Yes. You see, I wanted to ask you something. Cromwell left home last night and hasn't been back. He didn't come to see you, did he?"

"No," Liza quickly replied. "We haven't seen him for over a month."

"He mustn't know that Cromwell is here with us." The thought rang out in her head.

"He left home and hasn't come back. Everyone is looking for him. A report has been filed with the police."

"The police?" she said.

"Yes. I remembered that you were his friends. He told me your address some time ago, but I had forgotten the surname. I thought that perhaps he might have come here."

"No, Crom hasn't been back here since that night at the restaurant."

She shook her head.

He leant over her and she saw that he was smiling.

"Do you remember sticking your tongue out at me?"

"I was very angry with you. Forgive me."

He laughed.

"You're such a funny thing. I thought you were quite grown-up then, but you're really only a child."

"It was the dress."

"But I could tell straight away that you were very pretty."

She said nothing.

"What are you doing out in the garden so late? It's cold. You'll catch a chill. You should go home."

"I don't have my key. I can't get in. There isn't anybody at home, so I'm waiting for my brother to return."

He took her hand in his.

"You can't stay out here. It's too cold. Your hands are completely frozen already. Let's go to a café or something. We'll get you some grog to warm you up."

She shook her head.

"No, I have to wait for my brother."

"Then let's go and sit in the car, it's much warmer there."

She obediently followed him to the motor car and climbed in.

He wrapped a fur blanket around her.

"That's better, isn't it?"

"Yes, much better."

He switched on the light.

"Let's see what you look like then."

She lifted her worry-ridden face up to him.

"I look like this. Does it please you?"

"Terribly!" he said quite seriously. "What's your name?"

"Liza. Elizabeth."

"I'm going to call you Betsy. May I?"

She was still in a dream. The automobile, the black trees, the stranger in a grey coat. It was all a dream.

She shook off the blanket and ran her hand through her hair.

"Do sit still, you're cold as ice!"

She laughed. How easy it was to be carefree. She could no longer tell whether she was frightened or elated.

"I understand that Cromwell was in love with you." He paused. "I'm in love with you myself."

"So soon?"

"So soon."

She stretched out her legs and rested her feet against the side of the car. Slowly, she rolled down a stocking and pointed to a bruise on her knee.

"Look, I fell over yesterday. It hurts."

He leant over her legs.

"Won't you kiss it better?"

He touched her smooth, cold skin with his lips. She gently pushed his head away.

"That's enough. You can go now. If my brother comes back, I'll be in trouble."

"Is he very strict?"

"Horribly!" She jumped out of the car. "Goodbye now!"

He caught her sleeve.

"When can I see you again?"

"I don't know. You must go now," she insisted.

"Can I visit you tomorrow?"

"No."

"Then let's have dinner out tomorrow."

"No."

"Now look here." He reached into his wallet and extracted a calling card. "This is my address. Hide it. Call me and tomorrow we can go for lunch in some chic restaurant. Will you promise to call me?"

She slipped the card into her coat pocket.

"I promise. But you must go now."

"I'll be waiting. Goodbye."

The automobile pulled away.

The fog had cleared. The street lamp was on. A round white moon hung high in the sky. Liza's hands were cold.

The moon lit up the pink house. The pink shutters were shut, and the curtains in the upstairs windows were drawn.

"What can they be doing up there? Why can't I go indoors?"

She walked up to the porch.

"I'm cold. I'm going to ring."

But she didn't dare climb the steps to ring the doorbell.

"I'll wait a little longer."

Upstairs, a curtain twitched. A narrow yellow ray of light fell across the ground. Someone's face briefly appeared in the window before the curtain was drawn again. Liza lifted her head and looked up. But the curtain hung still.

"What's going on? How long do I have to wait here, and why?"

Suddenly the front door swung silently open. Nobody came out. The door stood open, revealing the dark hallway inside. All was still.

Liza stood there motionless, staring at the black rectangular hole.

"Come on, then," she heard a quiet voice say.

Slowly, she climbed the steps and passed through the door into the hallway. Nikolai was standing by the door. His shadow stretched all the way up to the ceiling.

"Close the door," he whispered. "Who was that?"

"It was Cromwell's cousin."

"What did he want? What did you say?" His frightened whispering continued.

"He wanted to know whether Crom had been here. I said that we hadn't seen him for six weeks."

"What else did he say?"

"Nothing."

"He didn't say that he'd be back tomorrow?"

"No."

"So he believed you?"

"Yes. Why is it so dark in here?"

"Hold on."

Nikolai turned the key in the lock and switched on the light. He was just as pale as before and he looked exhausted. His arms hung limply by his sides.

"Listen," he said hoarsely. "We're not going. That Cromwell changed his mind at the last minute. I gave him back the money and diamonds."

Liza clasped her hands to her breast.

"We're not going?"

"He refused to sign a document. We had an argument. He... he left."

"He left? But I didn't see him go."

"He used the back door."

Andrei appeared from the drawing room. His shirt collar was wide open. Damp hair stuck limply to his forehead.

"Go to bed, Liza," he said, without looking at her. "After all, you didn't get any sleep last night."

Liza started slowly climbing the stairs.

"Would you like some tea?" Nikolai called after her.

She didn't reply. She merely went faster.

In her room, she sat down in the armchair without even bothering to take off her coat.

"We're not going, we're not going, we're not going," she kept repeating. "It's all over. We're not going."

She heard footsteps on the staircase. They entered the adjoining room.

"It's fine," she heard Andrei say. "We can go to sleep now."

"No. We have to check the bathroom. I think there's still... Come on."

"I can't. I just can't. You go." Andrei's voice was breaking. "I can't any more." He was almost crying.

"It's all right, it's all right," Nikolai whispered. "Lie down and have a little rest. I'll go."

Footsteps descended the stairs. A strange sound could be heard amid the silence—the sound of factory workers scrubbing a shop floor.

Liza listened to the sound. "What is that? Should I go and look?" But she didn't move. "No, this has nothing to do with me. I must hold myself together." She clenched her hands into fists. "This has nothing to do with me." She drew her neck in, hiding in her coat like a snail in its shell. "This has nothing to do with me. I must go to bed," she thought. "I must go to bed, to sleep. I'm tired and I must sleep."

Without bothering to switch on the light, she got up and removed the velvet cover from the divan.

"I mustn't think of anything. I must sleep. I'm tired." She closed her eyes. "I'll count to a hundred, and then another hundred. I mustn't think of anything. Forty-five, forty-six, forty-seven… I must sleep."

"Liza," Nikolai called out quietly.

"What is it?"

Liza sat up. Her head was as clear as day, as if she hadn't been sleeping at all. Nikolai stood before her, wearing his pyjamas. The door to his room was wide open. A yellow lamp was shining on his desk.

"Liza dear, I'm sorry I woke you. I thought you were awake." Nikolai was smiling guiltily. "Andrei and I can't get to sleep. I thought you couldn't either. We're too on edge because of the trip and this whole saga."

He fell silent. Liza clasped her hands. She had to hold herself together. She mustn't be weak.

"Liza darling," Nikolai pleaded pitifully. "Come and sit with us, come and talk to us a little, Liza darling."

"Of course."

Liza got out of bed, threw a shawl over her nightdress and followed Nikolai in her bare feet.

Andrei was lying on the narrow divan, under the same chequered throw that Cromwell had used the night before.

"I've brought the little songbird to entertain us."

Nikolai lay down on the bed and pulled the duvet over himself.

"Make yourself comfortable at my feet, Liza darling."

Liza sat down and wrapped herself in the shawl.

"Well, Liza darling, tell us a story!" Nikolai asked.

"What kind of story?"

Nikolai laughed.

"What's with the tone? You sound like a schoolteacher. And your voice is very wooden. Are you angry that I woke you up?"

Liza shook her head.

"No, not angry."

"So what's the matter with you then?"

"I'm just very tired."

"You'll be back asleep in no time, no time at all. Don't be angry. We'll buy you a fox stole tomorrow. You've wanted one for a long time. We'll buy it tomorrow." Nikolai was pleading with her gently.

Liza was looking straight ahead, at the yellow lamp. Andrei lifted his head off the pillow.

"Don't be such a bore, Liza. Tell us a story."

"But I don't know what kind of story to tell you…"

"Oh, come on." Nikolai took her by the elbow. "You can think of something, you're so clever and such a good sport! Do you remember how you used to read me fairy tales at night when we were little?"

At this, Andrei perked up.

"You know fairy tales, Liza? Tell us a fairy tale. It doesn't matter which one—we just need to get to sleep."

Liza kept looking straight ahead.

"Very well."

"Come on then, come on," Andrei egged her on.

Nikolai rested his head back on the pillow.

"Liza, do you remember the one about Carrotine Leopardine? Do you remember that one?"

"I do, yes."

"Well, tell us that one."

Liza wrapped the shawl tighter around herself.

"All right, listen to this one. Once upon a time," she began in an even voice, "there lived a very important lady. She was called Carrotine Leopardine von Strippe. She was very important and very rich, and she kept her own horses. Her mother and father were rabbits. Ordinary grey rabbits. And she was ashamed of them. So one day…"

Liza carried on with the story of Carrotine Leopardine von Strippe and her rabbit parents, for a long, long time.

Nikolai was first to fall asleep. Liza turned her head.

"Andrei, are you asleep?" she whispered.

Andrei didn't answer.

She got up and tiptoed back to her room.

"Now I can go to bed, too. Now I can sleep, too."

She stretched out under the blanket and closed her eyes. She kept her hands clasped tightly, to hold herself together, to be strong, not to let on, even in her dreams.

XII

THE SOUND of a door slamming woke Liza up.

"Kolya!" she cried out. "Andrei!"

But all was still.

She got up, drew apart the curtains and looked out.

A yellow Citroën was parked by the garden gate. Andrei was crossing the garden, carrying a suitcase. His hat perched low over his brow and the collar of his coat was turned up. Nikolai was following him, hurrying along and continually glancing back over his shoulder. In his hand he carried a second tightly packed suitcase.

Liza watched as they placed the suitcases beside them in the back of the taxi, rather than in the front beside the driver. She watched the taxi pull away.

"Suitcases, suitcases," she thought, as her teeth chattered. "I must get dressed. I must leave. Wherever are my stockings?"

A feeling of anxiety made everything swim before her eyes. Her hands blindly groped at the divan.

"Where are my stockings? I can't go bare-legged."

She finally found the stockings and put on her dress and coat that were still draped over the armchair.

She was leaving. She needed only her shoes and hat.

All she had to do was run down the stairs, open the front door and she would be saved, she would be free.

She needed only a minute, just one minute more.

She dashed out of her room and ran downstairs. Her footsteps echoed loudly amid the silence. They didn't sound like her footsteps: they sounded like someone else's. Like those belonging to someone who was running after her, trying to get at her.

She glanced over her shoulder as she ran. There was nobody there; it was deserted all around. But she saw out of the corner of her eye a shadow on the white wall opposite the window—swaying black tree branches. They looked just like someone's hands. Just like Nikolai's hands. They were reaching out towards her, trying to get at her, trying to grab her throat, trying to strangle her.

She cried out, squeezed her eyes shut and ran on.

Her fleeting reflection flashed in the dark mirror in the hallway.

If only those hands didn't get at her. If only she had the strength to open the door. If only she didn't trip up.

Fear had made her heart almost stop. It was no longer beating, just barely whispering: "Run, run. If you trip, it will all be over." She couldn't catch her breath. "If I trip here, I'll die here."

She grasped the door handle.

"I know it. I won't be able to get out."

But the door opened easily.

Liza found herself on the porch. The sun shone brightly in her eyes. She descended the steps into the garden.

The garden gate creaked as it always did.

"Never in my life shall I set foot in this house again, never," Liza said out loud.

"Where am I going now? Who shall I go to? Odette is in Bordeaux. Who else is there?" she pondered. "Bunny!" The name suddenly popped into her head. "He's a kind-hearted soul. He'll help me."

She found two francs in the pocket of her coat. As she headed to the metro, she thought: "Bunny will help me."

It was a long journey. Bunny didn't live at the Claridge any more, but in a small pension on the boulevard Saint-Michel.

"Monsieur Rochlin is not at home," the owner announced from behind his desk.

"May I wait for him?"

He looked her over.

"You may."

Liza perched gingerly on the edge of the chair.

She didn't have to wait long. Soon enough Bunny came bounding towards her—plump, glowing and looking years younger. He had a cigar in his mouth and wore his bowler hat at a jaunty angle. His bulging, blue porcelain eyes glittered boldly behind his pince-nez.

He stopped in front of her and his lips drew into a smile.

"Liza darling?" He held a stumpy arm out to her and squeezed her hand in his. "Hello, Liza darling." He wasn't in the least surprised, as if they had seen each other only yesterday.

"Bunny, Bunny!" Liza squeezed his hand in hers. "Help me, Bunny."

He nodded.

"Of course, of course, I'll help," he said, pushing the bowler farther to the back of his head. "Here's what we'll do. You come with me—I've got a taxi waiting. You can tell me all about it on the way."

And with that, he turned back to the exit, without even going up to his room.

"Well, what's happened? Is it Natasha?"

Liza shook her head.

"No. Natasha is in Monte Carlo. Bunny, I've left home and I can never go back there, never."

The taxi cruised slowly along the embankment. Liza turned her face to the window and stared vacantly out at the Seine.

Bunny didn't ask any questions. He stroked her hand gently.

"Don't upset yourself, Liza darling. Things have a way of working out."

"Help me, Bunny. I don't have anyone in the whole world apart from you. I can never go back there."

"Of course, Liza darling. I'll help you. You were kind to me that day, do you remember? It was a terrifying day for me. I nearly died. I've made it through now, but back then… How could I forget? You were quite right to turn to me for help."

He paused to think for a moment.

"I'm leaving for Berlin today. I'm moving to Germany. I'll take you with me. You can be my daughter, Liza darling."

He embraced her and his eyes welled up with tears of joy.

"You'll be my daughter, Liza darling. My poor little orphan."

She leant against him.

"Will you really take me with you, Bunny?"

"We'll leave today. You've never been to Berlin? Everything's so neat and tidy there, you'll see. I'll take you to the zoo. You'll attend a German boarding school."

His talk grew faster and faster, inspired by his own benevolence.

Liza smiled as she listened to him.

"Will you really?"

"I'll make out a will in your favour."

Liza laughed.

"Bunny dear, you're too funny! Why the will?" She kissed him on the cheek. "You're so wonderful! Thank you. I'm so fond of you. I've always been fond of you. You know, once we were having lunch at Prunier's—and when they brought out my lobster, it looked just like you. It was looking up at us from its dish, just the way you always look at us from a taxi window. I couldn't eat it. I felt so sorry for it, as if it were you I would have had to eat."

Bunny joined in her laughter.

"Oh, Liza darling, we're going to live the life, just you wait and see!"

He looked at his watch and his face suddenly grew concerned.

"It's half past three already. There's one more place I must go. Liza darling, you can wait for me in a café and I'll come back to collect you."

He asked the driver to pull over and dived into a small café by the side of the road. Liza walked with him, holding his hand.

"You won't be long, will you, Bunny? I'd much rather go with you. I don't want to be on my own."

He turned to her. The look in his eyes was vague and cold again.

"No, you can't," he said sharply.

He sat her down by a window and, without asking her, ordered her a *bock*.

"I'll pay for it now, so you won't have to worry while you wait. I shan't be long. Have fun now."

He waved goodbye to her, and Liza was left all alone.

Was everything really going to turn out all right? Was she really going to live in Berlin with the kind, lovely Bunny?

She tried to picture Berlin in her mind's eye—broad straight streets with regular tall buildings on either side.

"Will Bunny's wife love me? Of course she will," she reassured herself. "I'll be as good as gold. She won't be able to help loving me. I'm so hungry. It would have been better if Bunny had ordered me a sandwich and a coffee rather than a beer. Never mind. He'll be back soon and he can get me something to eat then."

It grew dark. The street lamps came on. The clocks struck five, then six. Without thinking of anything in particular, Liza just watched the motor cars drive past.

"Bunny will be back any minute now."

But he didn't come.

The waiter studied the girl sitting in front of a full glass of beer with some curiosity.

Finally, he approached her.

"Are you waiting for someone, *mademoiselle*?"

"Yes, the gentleman who dropped me off here."

"I doubt he'll come now."

Liza raised her eyebrows in surprise.

"What do you mean, he won't come?"

"He must have forgotten, or perhaps something has prevented him…"

She shook her head resolutely.

"No, that's impossible. He'll be here any minute now."

When the clock struck seven, Liza got up.

"Where is your telephone?"

She found the number of Bunny's pension in the telephone directory.

"Monsieur Rochlin no longer lives here," she heard an accented voice say. "He and his wife left for Berlin an hour ago."

Liza hung up and slowly walked through the café towards the exit.

"What about the phone call?" a waitress behind the zinc bar shouted after her.

Liza put her last franc on the bar counter, before heading out into the street.

"What am I to do now? Where am I to go?"

She didn't spare Bunny a moment's thought. Bunny—just like everything that had happened on the previous day and overnight and that morning—vanished from her mind.

"What am I to do now?"

She stopped.

"What am I to do now?"

Vehicles drove up and down the streets. Pedestrians hurried home.

Home. All of them had homes to go to. But Liza had nowhere. She was homeless.

She looked around her. Was this really Paris? Paris, where she'd lived for so many years. No, it wasn't Paris. It was a strange, unfamiliar, unreal city.

People were walking down a wide street that was flanked by black leafless trees on either side. With each passing moment, there were fewer and fewer people. Their faces were pale and downcast, and their voices deadened. The dark, blind houses with their doors and windows tightly shut seemed lifeless. Street lamps shone dimly in the heavy blue light.

With each passing moment, there were fewer and fewer people, their voices grew quieter and the street lamps were extinguished one by one. Life left the city along with the noise and light. It soared up to the sky, animating it with stars and a large, blindingly bright moon that rolled over the clouds triumphantly.

The city seemed like a phantom. As did the people. Yes, these people were phantoms. They were only pretending to be in a hurry. They weren't alive—they were phantoms. If she were to walk up to one and say, "I'm hungry, please help me," the phantom wouldn't even turn to look at her. It wouldn't hear her. It would just smile absently and dissolve into the night.

She was alone in this enormous ghostly city. She had nowhere to go.

She was cold. She thrust her hands deep into the pockets of her coat. Her fingers felt something sharp.

"What's this?"

She extracted a visiting card.

"Leslie Grey, Hotel Majestic," she read under a street lamp.

Leslie Grey was the man who came yesterday. His name was Leslie Grey. She hadn't even known that.

"Leslie Grey," she said aloud, and suddenly, all became quite clear in her mind. She had to find this Leslie Grey. There was nobody else.

He had said to her: "When can I see you again? Promise that you'll write to me. I'm in love with you already." His eyes had shone. Yes, she could go to him.

The Hotel Majestic was on avenue Kléber, near the Étoile. How was she going to make her way there on foot, across the length and breadth of Paris?

Her feet grew heavy, her head ached and she had a horrible metallic taste in her mouth. She swallowed her saliva. "It's the hunger," she thought. "I haven't eaten anything today."

The streets seemed never-ending. She walked on and on. It felt as though she had been walking for days. She could hardly move her feet. She mustn't lose her way.

As she crossed a road that had been dug up for repairs, she tripped and fell. She could have stayed there on the ground, but she had to get up. Slowly, she got to her feet, rubbed her knee and carried on walking. She wiped her face: her cheeks were moist. That was when she realized that she was crying. She was crying, but she wasn't in pain. She wasn't in pain. There was no pain.

"That's enough of that. It'll pass," she reassured herself. She wasn't sure what exactly would "pass"—the grazed knee, herself or everything else.

At the Étoile, she was almost run over by a little motorcycle. She started running and came to a stop only when she had reached a large building with a terrace and spherical lamps outside. Palm trees and soft armchairs were arranged on the other side of large glass windows.

"This must be the Majestic."

A doorman set the revolving door in motion for her.

"Leslie Grey, please," she said to him.

The doorman called over another man.

"Mister Grey?"

"Number eighteen, on the first floor."

Liza followed him. In the lift, she felt as if she were suffocating. But it was over in a flash. Now she found herself walking down a broad corridor, scrutinizing the numbers on the doors. She arrived at number eighteen.

She knocked.

"Come in."

Leslie Grey was standing before a full-length mirror, wearing a white waistcoat and carefully doing up a white tie.

"Just put the jacket on the bed," he said without turning to look. "Thank you."

Liza leant against the wall. The mirror suddenly stretched out into a long gallery in front of her, with Leslie Grey somewhere at the end of it. Electric light bulbs rained fire down from the ceiling, right onto Liza.

"I've come to you," she struggled to utter, fighting back the weariness engulfing her, as a drowning man tries to fight off the waves. "I have nowhere else to go."

Part Four

I

L IZA WAS living in Normandy, in a hunting lodge.
Leslie Grey had taken her there the very next
morning.

The lodge stood in the middle of vast park grounds.
That spring was wet and windy.

Liza would wake up early and put on a light-blue
dress that had been bought off the peg in Rouen. She
would brush her hair; it had grown so long again here in
the countryside, where there was nowhere she could go
to have it cut. Then she would go through to the dining
room for breakfast. Leslie was sure to be there, sitting at
the table in his shooting jacket.

He would get up and kiss her on the cheek.

"Did you sleep well, Betsy?"

"Thank you, yes. And you?"

She would pour him some tea. He ate kippers, fried
eggs, porridge and orange marmalade.

"Please, help yourself," he would say. "You really must
put on some weight. It's no good being so thin."

Looking at him made her feel a little disgusted. The sight of the fish-head on the patterned plate and the smell of fried fat turned her stomach.

"Will you join me on the shoot today?"

"No, no," she would hurriedly refuse.

At that, he would laugh.

"Of course not, I knew it! When will you finally agree? You'll see how much fun it is to shoot hares. Yesterday, I came across a wild goat. I'd love to have some goat for dinner!"

He would get up and take his gun off the wall. The dogs would come running to him from the hallway, barking and whining with excitement.

Liza would stroke them and give them lumps of sugar to eat. She would then throw a cloak over her shoulders and walk Leslie to the park gates. That was the point at which she would turn back.

"Goodbye, Leslie. Happy shooting."

"Goodbye, Betsy. Don't miss me too much."

The sound of his cheerful whistling and the barking of the dogs carried to her for a while, but then Liza would be left in silence.

"Don't miss me." She didn't. She didn't miss anything. She didn't feel bored. Slowly, she would make her way back, along the sweeping avenue. A row of tall, erect linden trees flanked both sides. Narrow, shiny leaves were starting to cut through on the slender black branches. Liza imagined that someone could have painted them on. Over the pale-grey sky, clouds drifted past like plumes of smoke. Smoke rose up above the lodge like clouds. White doves sat on the roof. None of it seemed real. The park and the lodge might have been a stage set. Even the pale sun in the cloudy sky resembled a cut-out moon more than it did an actual sun. It was all so fresh, translucent, pale and quiet. Too pale, too translucent. It was all theatrically tender, theatrically sentimental—devoid of the burdens and hardships of life.

Liza raised her hand to the bright green leaves and caressed them. Somewhere far away, a gunshot rang out like a sigh. A fine mist was rising off the pond and up into the empty sky.

No, Liza was not bored. She regretted nothing, desired nothing, remembered nothing. She felt as if her soul were soaring up into the empty sky, like the smoke, over the trees, over the lodge. And this is why she could breathe so freely.

Geese swam in the pond. A frog croaked gently. In a pine forest, she came across a glade. The grass here was new and fresh. Nobody had walked on it until now. There was nobody to walk here, other than Liza.

"This is where the angels come down at dawn," thought Liza, vaguely recollecting her dream.

No, angels don't come down to earth. Why should they have to do that? They have their own business to take care of, up there in the heavens.

Liza turned off onto a path. A puppy came bolting towards her from the lodge.

"Toby! Toby!" she called out to him.

The puppy was only little. He was longhaired and ginger. She picked him up.

"How did you manage to come all this way? You must be tired!"

The puppy licked her hand and settled in her arms. She kissed him and pressed him to her breast.

"My little puppy, dear little puppy," she sang quietly. "My little puppy, dear little puppy."

She sat down on a bench. Tears were streaming down her face. She was crying and she didn't know why. She was neither sad nor bored. But there was an emptiness in her breast, as if her soul had left her body, like white smoke, to drift across the empty sky in clouds of white.

But she was not sad. Neither sad nor frightened. After all, she was to forget all about her past life. Indeed, she no longer thought about any of it. She never thought about Paris, or about her brother, or about Andrei. She never thought about *that time*: she never thought it through, she never really understood what had happened.

Maybe nothing had happened.

Nothing of her past life remained. She was different now, she was new. She wasn't even called Liza any more; she was Betsy. Why should Betsy have anything to cry over?

But the tears kept coming. They coursed down her face, cold and salty, and there was nothing she could do to stop them. Liza held the puppy closer. This puppy was the only thing in the world that she loved. She pressed her cheek into its soft fur.

What was he thinking about? What would he say if he could talk?

"I love grilled meat but I never get any."

No, he would say:

"I like being with you."

Liza smiled to herself and dried her eyes. "I wonder what he sees—does he see the same world as we do, or does he see everything differently?" She got up.

Back at the lodge, she went to her room and opened a book. "Mary has grey eyes," she read, "but John has blue eyes."

She repeated it aloud several times. Then she turned the page.

She studied one lesson a day, as set by Leslie, and in the evenings he would test her. In addition to this, they always spoke English to one another. Liza's English was still quite poor, but sufficient for conversations with Leslie.

Rain drummed against the window. Smoke billowed out of the fireplace. "What is the cabby doing with his handkerchief? He is sweating and using it to dry his face," read Liza. She closed her eyes.

This is it. This is her life now. It was never going to change. In six months' time, when she is fifteen and a half, Leslie will marry her and take her to England. But nothing will change. There will be twenty bedrooms in that house instead of the lodge's five, and the help will be a maid in black stockings and white gloves instead of the caretaker's wife. And there will be many more dogs there, and lots of horses. But it will all be the same. It will rain there, too, and Leslie will go out shooting there as well. And she will have to get up every morning, and she will have to make it through each day, and she will have to sleep through each night, until the morning. How many more such days and nights would there be?

She wasn't a girl any more, she was a grown-up. Her childhood had been unhappy, but being a grown-up was harder still. She was a grown-up now. It no longer mattered how old she was—fifteen, twenty or forty. Not now, not since that was how it was all going to be and there was no hope. But she wasn't complaining. What was there to complain about? So be it.

"What is the cabby doing with his handkerchief? He is sweating and using it to dry his face."

Outside, beyond the drizzle, the pond gleamed and the black branches swayed as the wide springtime sky stretched out above them.

11

UPON ARRIVING back from the shoot, Leslie Grey would go straight through to see Liza. His muddy boots left dirty prints on the floor.

"Look at the size of this one, Betsy!" he would say, brandishing a dead hare in front of Liza's face.

Blood dripped from the dead hare's face.

"Beautiful, isn't he? He'll be delicious with some beetroot salad!"

Liza would agree politely.

"Yes, beautiful. Yes, delicious."

After that, it was time to wash and change for dinner. Liza would put on her other grey dress. Leslie would exchange his shooting jacket for a dinner jacket and wait for Liza in the drawing room with its calico armchairs and peeling walls.

Liza would come in, her hair brushed straight.

He would get up to kiss her hand.

"Darling, you look most handsome tonight," he would say in a rather official tone.

"Dinner is served," the gardener would intone and throw the narrow door wide open.

That was his only job in the evenings.

Leslie would walk Liza in to dinner. She found it all quite ridiculous.

The caretaker's wife, wearing a white pinafore, would serve them onion soup.

At dinner they did not discuss shooting. Shooting was to be discussed over breakfast.

At dinner they would talk about their wedding and their future life together.

Leslie would pour himself some cider.

"You know, of course, that I'm a captain in the Scottish Rifles. We'll walk to the altar with my regiment's swords crossed above our heads. It's a grand and beautiful ceremony. They stand in a row, two men deep, and draw their swords high over their heads and the swords cross."

"Yes, that must be very beautiful."

"We've six months left in hiding. You know, sometimes I feel like a criminal who's kidnapped you. But what wouldn't one do for love?"

Liza nodded. He was speaking English and she didn't understand everything, but it was still good practice.

After dinner they would retire to the drawing room. Leslie would make himself comfortable by the fire.

"Let's have a little music," he would suggest.

Liza would obediently go over to the old, out-of-tune piano and sing 'Ol' Man River', which Leslie had taught her.

Her sad, gentle voice floated effortlessly up to the ceiling.

Leslie would smile in satisfaction.

"Excellent, my dear. You have a Negro's accent. And your singing's so melancholy, as if you'd spent your whole life on a plantation. Come to me, Betsy."

He would sit her on his lap and kiss the back of her head.

"Once we're married, it won't even take a year for you to forget that you were ever Russian, to forget your language. You'll be perfectly English."

Liza would nod. Yes, she had already forgotten everything. She was already English.

He would stroke her head.

"Your hair is growing out quite marvellously. Mother will approve. I do hope she won't object to our wedding. You're such a well-brought-up, demure girl; she'll like you. Yes, you're Russian, but your father was an officer in the Navy, wasn't he? And your grandfather was a general? Yes, I hope Mother won't have any objections."

He leant over her and kissed her neck. His cheeks blushed; his breathing grew heavy.

"Go over and sit on the chair please, Betsy. You're getting me too worked up, my darling."

He lit a cigar. In silence Liza watched the logs burning in the fire.

"It must run in the family—running away and hiding. Cromwell ran away, then I did. Maybe they've found him by now. I don't get any letters here after all. What do you think, Betsy? Do you suppose they'll have found him?"

Liza shook her head.

"I don't know."

It was possible that he had come back. She didn't know. She refused to think about it.

"If Cromwell's been found, he can be the best man at our wedding."

"Of course," Liza agreed.

There was nothing else to talk about. Leslie smoked in silence, stretching out his long legs in front of the fire.

The wind gently rustled the trees in the garden. The shutters creaked monotonously. A kerosene lamp with a green shade cast a pale light over the room.

The logs in the fireplace had almost burnt out. A blue flame danced over the embers.

Liza was too hot.

"I could go to bed now," she thought, looking at the door. But she couldn't find the strength to move. Her hands rested on her lap, and her eyes kept closing as she looked towards the door.

"It's going to rain tomorrow." The thought ran through her sleepy head. "The barometer dropped again today."

Quite unexpectedly, the door slowly and silently drew open, and Cromwell silently and slowly entered the room.

He walked in and stopped.

He looked just the same as he did in Paris, the last time she saw him. He was wearing the same blue blazer and yellow shoes. He was carrying a brass candlestick in his hand.

A draught made the flame on top of the tall candle flicker, casting a yellow glow over his pink cheeks.

He was tilting his head slightly to the side, looking cheerfully at Liza with his bright, pale eyes. His lips moved, as if he were about to speak, but he didn't say anything.

He just nodded at Liza, turned on his heels and, still smiling, walked out into the corridor holding the candle in front of him.

The door still lay open and a strong gust of air blew into the room.

"It's freezing!" exclaimed Leslie, turning around. "It's that damned door again!"

He jumped up and slammed the door angrily.

"It's so draughty here, the roof is bound to go flying off one of these days!"

He leant over Liza.

"Why are you staring at the door like that, Betsy? What's made you turn so pale?"

Liza transferred her gaze to him. Surely he'd seen Cromwell?

"What is it, Betsy? Did the draught frighten you?"

"No," Liza stuttered. "No, I'm not frightened."

"Go to bed, darling, you're practically asleep already."

At that, he lit a candle that was standing ready on the mantelpiece. A tall white candle in a brass candlestick, just like the one Cromwell had been holding.

"Come, Betsy, I'll see you to your room."

At the door to her room, he handed her the candle, kissed her hand, just as he always did, and, just as he always did, said: "Goodnight, Betsy. Lock the door and don't open it, even if I knock."

In reply, she said what she said every night: "Goodnight, Leslie. You know you'll never knock."

Then she walked into her room and ran her hand over her eyes.

"Crom's here. It must be true."

There could be no room for doubt. No longer could she fail to understand, fail to think it through. Everything was clear.

The gap in time disappeared. These never-ending two months, this new English life without any memories.

Time had suddenly shifted. The past had caught up with the present. It was yesterday. It was today. She heard the sound of a brush scrubbing the bathroom floor, she saw the heavy suitcases.

How could she have forgotten it, even for a minute? How could she pretend not to remember?

She was still holding the candle. Hot wax dripped onto her hand.

"I must go back at once. I must go back to Paris at once."

She placed the candle on top of the dresser and trained her ears. All was still in the lodge. Leslie must have gone to bed already.

She put on her hat and coat. In her coat pocket was a purse with one hundred francs. They were the hundred francs that Leslie had given her on the first day, so she should always have money on her. She hadn't broken the note. There was nothing to spend it on around here.

"That'll be enough for the journey."

She blew out the candle, opened the window, pushed open the shutters and jumped down into the garden.

The window wasn't very high up. Her dress snagged on a bush.

A large, round green moon was swimming across the sky. Liza lifted her face to look at it.

"Like the lamp in the drawing room." The vague thought crossed her mind.

The black shadows of trees danced across the grass. The clouds condensed and scattered as they drifted across the moon.

Liza walked over to the pond. The moon swam out from behind a thick black cloud and came to a standstill over the tall tops of the fir trees, right above the pond. The moon's reflection fell into the pond—round, shimmering, bright. It made everything brighter. Much brighter. So much brighter and completely silent.

Liza passed under the black arch of the gateway. She knew that it was made of red brick, but right now it seemed black. The cold, bright moonlight drained the colour from everything, leaving just black and white. Everything was either black or white.

White signs with black traffic markings. Black rocks lining the sides of a straight, wide white road. And on top of the hill, by the junction, a tall black cross—a monument to those who fell in the war.

Everything was so far, yet so clearly visible. As if it were daytime. Clearer than in daytime.

Liza wasn't afraid. She felt as if someone's guiding hand were carrying the round green lamp through the clouds, so that she, Liza, should have light. So that she should not lose her way.

In the distance she saw black-and-white buildings.

Here was the town, here was the railway station.

III

L IZA WAS SITTING in a third-class carriage. Across from her were three peasants, and beside them a parish priest who in a quiet whisper was reading prayers from a small black prayer book.

Liza stared at the darkness through the window. She'd made it just in time, she wasn't too late. Tomorrow morning she was going to be in Paris.

She could hear a clucking coming from a basket on the top shelf.

"I've got a hen in there," a fat peasant woman explained to her neighbours. "I'm taking it to Paris as a gift for my son. They don't know what a real plump hen is in Paris!"

The hen captured everyone's attention.

"Why don't you let her out for a walk," said the old man who was smoking a pipe. "She doesn't want cooping up in that basket."

The peasant woman readily agreed. The hen came down from the shelf.

"See how plump she is! Go on, pinch her breast. I've brought her up on nuts!" the peasant woman fussed.

The feathers on top of her colourful hat shook.

Her round eyes looked about with a proud gaze. Her aquiline nose seemed ready to peck.

"Here, pinch my hen!"

A multitude of hands reached out towards the hen. Even the curé momentarily lifted his eyes from his prayer book.

The peasant woman politely offered her hen to Liza, as if it were a box of chocolates.

"Would you like to pinch her, *mademoiselle*?"

Liza looked at the peasant woman.

"No, thank you." She turned back to the window.

The carriage was hot and filled with smoke. One by one the passengers fell asleep. Loud snoring joined the beating of the wheels. The hen, its legs tied, jumped helplessly around the floor, flapping its wings.

Liza closed her eyes. Three hours to Paris.

IV

I T WAS A COLD and windy morning in Paris. Porters were busy, carrying luggage. Taxis were coming and going. Passengers stood on the steps, peering around with that baffled provincial look with which even those who leave Paris for only a short while inevitably return.

Liza left the station, crossed the square and descended into the metro. She didn't lift her head or look around once. She had no interest in the motor cars, the people or the buildings. It was as if she hadn't been away for two months, but rather had just stepped out to buy some bread for breakfast and was now hurrying home.

Liza rushed along the quiet streets of Auteuil. Here was their local creamery on the corner, and here was the pharmacy. Her head was empty. She was almost running. Through the bright green trees, a pink house suddenly came into view, almost unexpectedly. Liza stopped and placed her hand on the garden gate. The garden was overgrown. The garden paths hadn't been swept. The shutters were closed. They were still asleep. The garden gate creaked as it always did, like a cat meowing.

Liza climbed the porch steps and rang the doorbell.

Nobody opened the door. Her heart skipped a beat. They've left. She rang again. The ringing was urgent and shrill. They've left.

She lifted her head and looked up at the windows. The curtains were drawn. In the far window, she saw a curtain twitch, just as it had done that night, and she caught a glimpse of a pale face on the other side of the windowpane. The curtain quickly drew shut again, and soon she heard the sound of familiar footsteps. The key turned in the lock twice, the chain fell with a clank and the door opened.

"Andrei!"

"Liza, is that you?"

He grabbed her by the hand, pulled her into the hallway and locked the door after her.

"Liza, you've come back?"

It was very dark in the hallway. Andrei leant over her, staring at her intently.

It was as if he didn't believe that it was really her. His hand squeezed hers tightly.

His eyes shone feverishly.

"Is that you, Liza? Have you come back?"

He gave a sharp laugh. The sound echoed in the silence.

Liza started. For some reason she felt uneasy. She turned to look at the locked door behind her.

"It's locked, I can't get away now. Like a mouse in a mousetrap," she thought. "But even if it were open, I would never leave."

Andrei helped her to take off her coat and led her through into the dining room.

The shutters were closed. The light was on, casting a yellow circle on the tablecloth. Everything was in disarray. Nobody had cleaned the place for a long time.

Andrei had a new manner of walking—a careful, prowling step; he never used to walk like that. He was still holding Liza's hand.

Liza looked at him without saying a word. Why had she come here? She wanted to find something out, but what? Not a single question came to mind. She had no thoughts. Her head was empty.

"Sit down, have some coffee." Andrei placed a cup in front of her. "It's still hot, I've only just brewed it."

Without thinking she sat down and took a sip of coffee. It seemed to her that she couldn't taste it at all, but for some reason she said:

"It's too sweet."

"I'll make another cup," he fussed. "Hold on, I'll be right back."

"Never mind, it doesn't matter."

"But it'll only take a minute."

"I don't mind. I'll drink this one."

He sat down beside her.

"You know, I've been thinking about you for days, calling out to you in my mind. I'm so happy that you made it, that you're not too late!" he was speaking quickly, in a rasping, hushed voice.

"Not too late for what?" she wanted to ask, but fear stopped her.

Andrei took her by the hand again.

"Where have you been all this time?"

"In the countryside. With Cromwell's cousin."

Andrei registered no surprise.

"Did you like it there?"

Liza shook her head.

"Not really."

He asked no more questions.

He just said: "But you'll have to go back to him in the end."

"Why?" she wanted to ask, but again she was too frightened.

By now she had grown used to the closed shutters and the electric light. In essence, nothing had changed here, save that it was in greater disarray, dusty everywhere, and the air was stagnant and damp.

Liza looked at the old familiar divan. How many evenings she had spent here, just like this—with Andrei, under this light. And Andrei was almost the same as he always was. Only he was a little thinner, a little more anxious. In essence, everything was very nearly the same as always; she was trying to convince herself, knowing that nothing was the same.

"Liza," said Andrei, pressing his cheek into her shoulder, "I'm so glad that you've come back, that you caught me in time."

He paused briefly. A twitch contorted his face.

"What was that?" she thought, frightened. "Where did that come from? He never had that before."

Andrei closed his eyes.

"I feel so calm with you here. I could sleep like this. You know, I hardly sleep now."

She stroked his hair.

"Where's Nikolai?"

"He's in Brussels." Andrei lifted his face to hers. He was excited. "Brussels was splendid. We went to Ostend to try our luck. I had some luck at first, but then I lost everything. That's when we went back to Brussels. Brussels is splendid."

"So why did you come back?"

He cast a glance over his shoulder towards the door.

"We left his coat here."

"Coat? What coat?"

"*His* coat. We forgot to burn it. It might have been found. We burnt his suit, but we forgot the coat."

He held her tighter, as if wanting to protect her.

"Don't worry, they won't do anything to you. You didn't know anything."

She shook her head slowly.

"It's not me I'm worried about."

"When I left," he hastened to continue, "Nikolai ran out of cash. He wanted to sell the pearls and that's when they caught him. I read about it in the papers."

He paused for breath.

"It's all over now."

"It's all over," she repeated quietly, neither confirming nor questioning what he'd said.

They sat at the table, holding each other closely. His head rested on her shoulder. After a sleepless night on the train, she wanted to lie down and stretch out. The electric light shining in her face was blinding.

"Liza," he said, squeezing her hand in his, "I should send you back to him right away, but I can't. Please. Be kind to me. You're my angel after all, my angel of solace. Stay with me today, until the last train." He pressed his lips to her hand. "Unless you're afraid, Liza?"

She covered his mouth with her hand.

"Hush. I'm not leaving you."

He leant over her and looked at her with his bright begging eyes.

"You'll stay with me until the evening? Do you promise?"

"I promise."

His pale cheeks flushed pink. He got up and took down a guidebook from the sideboard, the same one that Cromwell had leafed through on the last night.

"What's the name of the station you need?"

"Vieux Rouen."

The pages rustled.

"The last train is at ten-thirty."

Andrei turned his anxious face towards her. His lips were spread in a smile. He looked at the clock.

"It's ten now, Liza. We have the whole day ahead of us, Liza. A whole day!"

He was choking with excitement.

"Just don't think about anything. Forget about it all. We're going to spend the whole day together!"

He began pacing the room feverishly.

"I'm sorry it's such a mess here. You must think it's a disgrace. And the light's on, as if it were night-time. Hold on, I'll make us comfortable."

He opened the windows, pushed open the shutters and switched off the light.

The grey light of morning flooded the room. Andrei winced.

"What a miserable rainy day! But wait…"

He pulled the yellow silk curtains together and the light filtering through them became sunny and warm.

"And here's the sunshine! Can you see it? The sky is blue and the sun is out. Out there in the garden the lilacs are in full bloom and the larks are singing." He spoke rapidly. "You can't see it, because the curtains are drawn, but if we were to open them, it would get too hot."

He turned to look at Liza, smiling.

"What a wonderful day it is today! It's our day. We have to be happy and carefree."

Liza made herself comfortable on the divan.

"That's right, completely carefree. Come and sit with me. Today is just as wonderful as the day we first met. Do you remember it?"

He sat down beside her.

"Of course, I remember! You were wearing a white dress and your hair was down and your eyes were big and blue. I didn't like you that much, you looked too much like a doll. We were playing tennis and the ball hit your breast and you cried out, and I thought I'm going to fall in love with this girl—and then I was angry with myself."

Liza smiled.

All of a sudden she could believe in the sunshine and skylarks outside the window. She felt happy and carefree. There was nothing—no past, no present. Nothing but happy childhood memories.

"It was a Thursday in September, in the Bois de Boulogne. I was twelve," she interrupted him. "I liked you straight away. You were so serious. I even grew to respect Kolya when I realized he had friends like you."

But Andrei wanted to speak, too, to prove that he too hadn't forgotten anything.

"By the time I was first invited to your house, I was already in love with you."

They were sitting on the divan, holding hands and looking into each other's eyes, speaking over one another.

"I thought that you lived in such luxury! You entertained me and served me hot chocolate, just like a little hostess. I was so embarrassed. And Jim almost bit me then!"

"Jim? You remember Jim?"

"Do you remember when I told you I loved you?"

Liza raised her eyebrows.

"Of course I remember! It was when Lindbergh landed, it was a Saturday in May."

"That's right! It was so windy and everyone said that he'd break his neck, that he was a madman. We couldn't get to Le Bourget, we had no money. We walked up and down the boulevards that night. You were so worried! And then do you remember what happened when the news spread that he'd landed, all the celebrations? I said, 'Congratulations, Liza.' Everybody was cheering, and so were we."

Liza smiled again.

"Yes, we cheered so much!"

"I was shouting, 'I love you Liza'—and you heard me and you shouted, 'I love you, too, Andrei.' Do you remember? And that's when we shared our first kiss. Do you remember?"

"And the very next day we bought a huge portrait of Lindbergh and hung it over my bed, so I should always be reminded of you. How silly we were!"

"Were? Aren't we still silly?"

Liza embraced him.

"Well, yes, we're just as silly now. And I love you just as much."

"I love you even more, Liza. You know, you're the only one I've ever loved. It's just that sometimes… How can I explain it?… Sometimes I wondered whether I hadn't dreamt it all up—you and my love for you. As if you didn't even exist. I would look at you, but I wouldn't see or hear you. Do you understand me?"

Liza frowned in concentration.

"No, I don't understand. How is that possible?"

"I don't understand it myself now. But it would happen so often back then. And I'd get so jealous!" He paused. "I was jealous of *him*," he added quietly.

She shook her head.

"Don't bring that up. Like you said, we're just like we were back then. We're so carefree, so happy. We're such children."

"That's right, we're children. You're twelve and I'm fourteen, and we're playing at round-the-world adventure."

He was excited again.

"Liza. We're in China. How do you like this rice paddy?"

Liza looked around.

"I like it a lot. I like everywhere, so long as you're with me. But this rice paddy needs a clean, and you, mister Chinaman, need to brush your hair."

She got up.

"What about lunch? The Chinese like to eat, too."

"I won't be a minute. We've only bread and cheese in the house. I shouldn't go outside…"—a twitch contorted his cheek again.

Liza interrupted him.

"You don't have to go outside. I'll go and buy everything we need. Lay the table while I'm out. I have money."

Andrei held out fifty francs to her.

"Here, take this as well. It's all I have left, but I shan't need it any more."

Liza slammed the door shut behind her and quickly made her way down the garden path.

"How cold it is! It's not summer at all. There aren't any flowers or sunlight."

A grey cloudy sky sat low over the rooftops.

At the corner, right beside their garden fence, she saw a moustachioed man wearing a black coat and a black bowler hat. He studied her intently.

Her hands grew cold.

"No, it's nothing. It's just someone out for a walk. Why shouldn't he be walking here?"

She passed him, her legs trembling. He didn't seem to notice her.

But when she left the shop, she found him standing in front of the window, closely inspecting a display of canned goods.

The heavy shopping bag weighed her arm down. She glanced carefully over her shoulder. The moustachioed man was following her slowly.

Hardly breathing, she ran up the porch steps and rang the doorbell. The door opened instantly.

"So fast, Liza dear? You're out of breath!"

"I wanted to be home with you as quickly as possible."

Andrei took the bag from her hand.

"There's such a lot here! Wasn't it difficult to carry?" She was still breathing heavily.

"No, but I ran. It's so nice in our home, but outside it's cold and horrible."

"Did you see anyone?" he asked concernedly.

Liza took off her coat.

"No, no one. Oh no, wait, let me think… I did. I saw one cat and two rooks."

Andrei had managed to brush his hair and change into a new suit that Liza hadn't seen before.

Liza looked him up and down.

"You're so dapper, Andrei! Let's go and have lunch."

The dining room was clean and tidy and the table had been laid. Andrei opened the shopping bag.

"I'm glad you came back so quickly. Without you here, I felt frightened again."

Liza stroked his hair.

"Don't, don't," she said hastily. "Look what I've bought!"

They sat at the table, facing one another, all the better to see each other.

Liza served herself some chicken.

"I've never eaten such delicious chicken before!"

She raised her glass.

"I've never drunk such delicious wine before!"

"And I've never seen your smile so beautiful and your eyes so bright before!"

She laughed, shaking her head. Her fair hair fell around her forehead.

"It's because I'm happy." She paused to think. "You know, Andrei, I read somewhere that when Goethe was old, someone asked him how much of his life had been happy. He answered, 'Seven minutes.' I've been happy for four hours already, from the very second I set foot in here this morning. It's enough to last a lifetime. Maybe it's even too much."

She sighed.

"This kind of happiness is hard to bear. It's too much. You're happy, too, aren't you?"

He nodded his head in silence. His face was turned to the window. His dark eyes shone brightly and his lips were drawn in a smile. Light fell across his blushing cheeks. It seemed as if they were glowing with happiness, strength and youth.

"You're so young!" she said with sadness.

He laughed.

"You're two years younger than I am!"

"That's right, and I've always thought you were older, but now I can see that you're still a boy. Pour me some more wine."

She smiled as she drank. Her head hung wearily.

"Oh, I am so happy, so very happy," she sighed.

He leant across the table.

"Are you tired?"

She placed her arm on the table and laid her head on top of it.

"Frightfully tired."

"You ought to lie down."

"No, no, I mustn't sleep. I don't want to miss a single moment. We have so little time left."

"You can lie down without going to sleep. Come, rest in bed."

He helped her to her feet.

She spotted a blue envelope lying on top of the sideboard. She recognized Natasha's handwriting.

"I almost forgot—that letter's for you."

Liza tore open the envelope.

"*My darling children,*" she read, "*take care of yourselves and study hard. I've lost a little bit of money here, so they won't let me leave the hotel. But I'll be back soon! If you've run out of money, Kolya is to go and ask Bunny, and I'll…*"

Liza put the letter back on the sideboard without finishing it.

The shutters in the bedroom were closed.

"It's nice in here, as dark as if it were night."

The fresh embroidered sheets radiated a cool white light on the low bed.

"Did you make up the bed?" she asked him in a whisper.

"I thought you might be tired after your journey," he answered just as quietly.

"I've never slept in this bed before."

"Lift up your arms."

Slowly, he took her dress off over her head.

"Now give me your foot."

He kneeled in front of her.

"No, wait, I need to wash."

"All right, but let's go together."

Her bare shoulders glistened in the darkness. He put his arms around her.

"How thin you are!"

Liza opened the bathroom door and switched on the light.

The bathroom looked the same as it had always done, and it had the same damp smell that it always had. "A damp, boggy, toady smell," she remembered.

She kept her eyes facing forward, trying not to look at the floor. What if there was still blood there? But the floor had been scrubbed clean and each of its grey tiles gleamed.

Liza turned the tap and picked up the sponge. Water ran down her back and her arms. It was cold and tickled her. And she got a cold, ticklish, sad feeling in her chest. Liza shuddered from the cold and the sadness. Her ears were ringing and her head was spinning.

"I'm drunk," she thought, as she lathered her shoulders.

Andrei was standing next to the small gas boiler.

"See, it's so simple." His voice was very quiet. "You turn the gas on like this and leave the door open."

Panicked thoughts darted around her head. She felt afraid again. She pretended not to have understood.

She passed him a towel.

"Would you rub my back down?"

He started drying her with the towel.

"You're ready."

They went back to the bedroom. Liza threw off her slippers and lay down on the wide bed. She moved over to the very edge. Blood kept throbbing in her ears.

"You know, I'm drunk," she said.

"Don't worry, it'll soon pass."

Liza could hear him hurriedly undressing.

"It'll soon pass."

He pulled back the covers and lay down beside her. His knees brushed against her.

"How thin you are!" he said again and placed his arms around her.

She let out a deep sigh. His face leant over hers, his lips touched her lips. She wanted to get away, to break free.

"Liza, why are you scared of me? Are you scared of me?" he whispered right into her ear.

Frightened, she was trying desperately to fend him off. "Let go."

"Why are you scared of me? Were you scared of *him* too? And the other ones?"

"I've never—"

"What do you mean, never?" he interrupted her. "What about the night *he* spent with you? And this new one?"

"I've never," Liza said again, "not with anyone."

"You're lying." He let go of her, "but if you don't want to, if you're scared of me, then we don't have to."

She put her arms around him.

"You don't believe me, Andrei? I love you. And I'm not scared at all."

He leant over her again.

"Liza."

Now she was lying next to him, with her eyes closed. Through the ringing in her ears, she could hear his excited voice.

"Liza, I'm so happy! You know, I was so tortured, I was so jealous. Liza, I'm so happy now."

She smiled at him, her eyes still closed.

"I'm happy, too." She wanted to tell him, to explain it all to him—all her life, all her love, but she just said: "I'm happy it happened today. With you."

"Liza, I'm so grateful to you. Now, I'm completely happy."

He was kissing her head, her hair, her breasts.

She didn't say anything in return. He rested his head on her shoulder.

"Here, with you, I could sleep."

Suddenly he lifted his head again.

"Liza, do you realize…?"

She opened her eyes and studied his anxious face in the half-light.

"Liza, you could have a child." He paused for a moment, as if lacking the strength to go on. "Think about it, Liza, a child—our child." He was whispering hurriedly. "Promise me, promise me that you won't do anything. Let him be born. You'll be able to look into his eyes and think of me. Our child."

"A child," she repeated quietly, and recollected how Cromwell had slept on her shoulder, just like a child, like her child. Her heart leapt with pity. Pity for the murdered Cromwell and pity for her child who would never be born, mixed with pity for Andrei. She let out a sigh and tears streamed down her face.

"You're crying, Liza. Why?"

She smiled through her tears.

"Everyone must cry when they're too happy."

He passed her his glass of wine.

"Drink this."

She drank obediently and the ringing in her ears grew even louder. Through the haze, she saw Andrei's pale face leaning over her.

"I love you," she whispered.

Liza opened her eyes. She found herself in a narrow boat, floating down a black river. A white sail was hanging over the side. No, it wasn't a boat, it was a bed and the sail was a bed sheet. But there were still huge white ostrich-feather fans swaying above her head and music was coming from somewhere in the corner of the room.

"Andrei," she called out.

And suddenly Andrei's face swam out of the darkness.

"Andrei, I love you."

Andrei lit a match and fished his watch out from under his pillow.

"It's a quarter to eight. We have a whole two hours left."

The match was extinguished and everything merged together again. Andrei's arms held her tightly and his lips kissed hers.

"Liza, I love you. I'm happy." Andrei whispered into her ear, "Liza, Liza, wake up. We only have two hours left after all. Only two hours."

Liza came to. The room was silent and dark. Andrei was asleep. She was lying on her back. Her head hurt and her back hurt and she couldn't move from pain, weakness and fatigue.

"It's as if I've been hit by a tram," she thought sleepily.

There was a ringing in her ears and her head was empty. But she knew one thing. She knew she must get up.

"You must get up. If you don't get up, you'll fall asleep, and then… Then…" She shuddered. "You must get up right now. You must."

Carefully, she sat up, and carefully, she placed her feet on the floor. Everything swam before her eyes as pain ran through her body.

Liza staggered to her feet, holding on to the headboard for support as she made her way unsteadily to the bathroom.

"I must." She flicked the switch and stood still, shielding her eyes from the bright light.

Then she walked over to the gas boiler and turned the handle.

"How simple."

After turning out the light, she made her way back to the bed in the dark.

Andrei held his arms out towards her in his sleep.

"Liza, Liza, where are you?"

She lay down next to him.

"Sleep. Sleep now. I'm here, right here, beside you."

He put his arms around her and held her to him as he slept.

She rested her head on his shoulder and blissfully closed her eyes. Somewhere nearby, just below the window, she heard a motor car sound its horn. But nothing from that hostile, frightening, strange world could hurt them now.

PUSHKIN PRESS

Pushkin Press was founded in 1997, and publishes novels, essays, memoirs, children's books—everything from timeless classics to the urgent and contemporary.

This book is part of the Pushkin Collection of paperbacks, designed to be as satisfying as possible to hold and to enjoy. It is typeset in Monotype Baskerville, based on the transitional English serif typeface designed in the mid-eighteenth century by John Baskerville. It was litho-printed on Munken Premium White Paper and notch-bound by the independently owned printer TJ International in Padstow, Cornwall. The cover, with French flaps, was printed on Rives Linear Bright White paper. The paper and cover board are both acid-free and Forest Stewardship Council (FSC) certified.

Pushkin Press publishes the best writing from around the world—great stories, beautifully produced, to be read and read again.

STEFAN ZWEIG · EDGAR ALLAN POE · ISAAC BABEL
TOMÁS GONZÁLEZ · ULRICH PLENZDORF · JOSEPH KESSEL
VELIBOR ČOLIĆ · LOUISE DE VILMORIN · MARCEL AYMÉ
ALEXANDER PUSHKIN · MAXIM BILLER · JULIEN GRACQ
BROTHERS GRIMM · HUGO VON HOFMANNSTHAL
GEORGE SAND · PHILIPPE BEAUSSANT · IVÁN REPILA
E.T.A. HOFFMANN · ALEXANDER LERNET-HOLENIA
YASUSHI INOUE · HENRY JAMES · FRIEDRICH TORBERG
ARTHUR SCHNITZLER · ANTOINE DE SAINT-EXUPÉRY
MACHI TAWARA · GAITO GAZDANOV · HERMANN HESSE
LOUIS COUPERUS · JAN JACOB SLAUERHOFF
PAUL MORAND · MARK TWAIN · PAUL FOURNEL
ANTAL SZERB · JONA OBERSKI · MEDARDO FRAILE
HÉCTOR ABAD · PETER HANDKE · ERNST WEISS
PENELOPE DELTA · RAYMOND RADIGUET · PETR KRÁL
ITALO SVEVO · RÉGIS DEBRAY · BRUNO SCHULZ · TEFFI
EGON HOSTOVSKÝ · JOHANNES URZIDIL · JÓZEF WITTLIN